# The Periodic Coffee House

Steve Cain

# The Periodic Coffee House

*The Periodic Coffee House* is a work of fiction. References to actual persons, places, happenings have been fictionalized. All characters and incidents come from the author's imagination and are not intended as real.

The author maintains full ownership and/or legal rights to publish this work.

Cover design and production by Steve Cain.



More from Steve Cain:

The Great Inevitable, Losantiville Press
Jumpin' Jesus, Hallelujah, Amazon
Thorn, Amazon
The Box of Dreams and Memories, Amazon,
Leave a Message, Amazon,
December Promise, Amazon
The Crow and the Harp, Amazon
Nothing but Sand, Amazon
Dead Birds, Amazon
Bombs and Dragons, Amazon
My Guardian Anger, Amazon
The Silent Shore, Amazon
Your Name is Sin, Amazon
Tracks and Traces, Amazon
Through the Rainy Windshield, Amazon

The Periodic Coffee House

# DEDICATION

This book is dedicated to my son, Ethan Cain. He has been my biggest fan and has been waiting for this book to come out for a long time. I love you, bud!

# CONTENTS

# ACKNOWLEDGMENTS

I'd like to thank my wife and kids for allowing me to take the time to pursue writing and playing in bands. I know that's time that I take away from them, and I hope they think it's worth it.

# <u>Author's Note</u>

The stories found in this collection are centered around a fictional river village town called Nevileville.  It is kind of a cross between Augusta, Georgia, where I grew up, and New Richmond, Ohio, where I currently live.  The people in these stories are also fictional, although a good bit of what is written about is autobiographical.  These were written between 2016 and 2018.

Many of these stories were written with no theme in mind.  As I wrote, some commonalities came out, and decided to edit some of the stories so that they had continuity.  I thought about Stephen King, my favorite write, and how many of his stories are set in Maine around a fictional town called Castle Rock.  Some of these stories were originally set in Georgia, and I changed these so that the setting was in Ohio.  Both Augusta and New Richmond are river towns, so it wasn't much of a stretch.

The periodic table idea started in the story "Cilly."  The story begins in a coffeehouse that had a periodic table on the wall, which is kind of strange for a coffeehouse.  In high school, I was in the Science Club and Science Team, and I thought I wanted to be a pharmacist.  My chemistry teacher, Mrs. Croft, had a large periodic table on her wall, as probably most chemistry teachers do.

I wrote "Memorial Day," in 2016.  It is about a town that had a unique way to deal with and remember their dead.  I later referenced this event in "The Periodic Coffee House."

"The Savior in the Coffee House" drove me to add all these stories into the same "universe."  I realized I had already written a couple of stories about coffee and coffee houses, and rather than have someone think I was just rewriting the same story, I decided to have these stories just mesh together and tell tales about the people that inhabited this coffeehouse.  You know there are all kinds of stories. If walls could just talk!  The barista in the story was referenced in "The Periodic Coffee House," and I decided to tell her own story in "Lucy."

"RIP Andy Sizemore-A Life in Signs" came about one morning while I was driving to work.  Most times we never think about all the road signs there are, and I wondered how many were on my drive to work.  There was a lot!  You always see little memorials to people who have had accidents on the road, but you never know their story. Here's one where you do find out the story.

The Firecracker Bunch was originally set in Augusta, Georgia.  There is a real place that was an aqueduct, or what locals called the "Achy Docks."  It was a place where water could be released from Lake Olmstead or the Augusta Canal into the Savannah River.  I used to go fishing and swim in that area.  Anyway, this story was based on another writing prompt that had to do with the 4th of July.  What better for the 4th of July than fireworks?

"The Periodic Coffee House" was my attempt to begin bringing these stories together.  I wanted to introduce the village and how the coffee house got started.  It introduced "A Portal through Pages," which is another village story that has yet to be written.  It introduced "Miss American Pies," which I thought was a nice little homage to the Don MacLean song.  The story also introduced "Gutterball," which was a real duck that we used to feed at Lake Olmstead in Augusta.  He really was missing part of his bill.

So welcome to Nevileville, the village that never was, that was, and then was no longer.  I hope you enjoy your visit.  Love and be loved, and be the blessing!

# As I Walked by the River, A Beginning

As I walked by the river,

So much beauty did I see,

A sweet, blue-feathered peacock,

Quacking ducks and honking geese.

Azure skies, reflected sun

On swiftly flowers waters,

Parents walking hand in hand

With little sons and daughters.

Store front pastels orange and pink,

Others yellow, blue, or green.

A record store, a butcher,

And a coffeehouse between,

A book store and a pie shop;

Many goodies in the town.

The wonders of the village,

Sure to turn frowns upside down.

We gather in the town's square

For picnics and fireworks,

Concerts, plays, and movies are

Some of our village's perks.

There's nothing like our village,

Full of wonder, filled with pride

Our Nevileville, our village,

Here along the riverside.

# The Periodic Coffee House

Sam Keller finished whipping his latte and took a sip. The coffee went down his throat and warmed his stomach. "Umm, that's good," he said. He took a look around the empty coffeehouse. He was going to miss this place. There were a lot of memories here. There was the periodic table that hung on the north wall. It had belonged to his father and had been hanging there for over 40 years. Over the years people had decorated it with little drawing and cartoons. Some had signed their names or written verse on it. Someone had even drawn a red heart around element #74. Tungsten, chemical symbol W. Why someone would do that was beyond him, but people always surprised him. There was a picture on the east wall over one of the tables. It was of a mallard duck that lived in the area. His daughter had named it Gutterball because it was missing part of its top bill. Why his daughter chose the name Gutterball was another mystery. She had been 8 years old at the time. There was also a framed 4" x 6" picture sitting on the counter next to the register. The picture was of his former barista, Lucy, and a bearded man with long hair that she had said was an actor on a television show. It was such a horrible thing that happened to her.

The front door and windows looked out onto the river. This was one of Sam's favorite places in the world. He could come and sit and look out when they weren't busy serving coffee. The area to the right of the door was a cleared off spot they had used for poetry readings, acoustic performances, and open mic nights, but not anymore. As Don McLean had said, "the man there said the music wouldn't play." The music had died. For all of them.

Sam's father, Ike Keller, had opened The Periodic Coffee House in 1977.  Ike had been a chemist at a Research and Development facility for 20 years, and the company stock had boomed.  Ike had taken a buyout package from the company and thought he would take an early retirement.  He was too fidgety, however, and took a position as a chemistry teacher at the high school.  He taught class for 5 years, long enough to draw a pension from the state.  For a couple of years, he had been thinking about opening a coffeehouse in the village.  There was nowhere in town to get a good cup of coffee and to socialize.  There was just a fast-food restaurant and a bar, and Ike saw a need.  He had been researching during those couple of years to see what it would take to open up his own business, and now was the perfect time.  An old riverfront building had come up for sale.  It had been a dry goods store during the late 1800s and later a tavern from the early 1900s to about 1954.  It had been vacant since then, and the owner finally decided to let it go.  It needed some work and some TLC, and Ike was just the man for the task.  He cleaned it up, fixed it up, and took his periodic table from the classroom with him.

Ike had called his shop The Periodic Coffee House.  He thought it was an interesting name, and it played on his chemistry background.  He also liked the slogan he had come up with: "We drink coffee…periodically."  It was a testament to Keller's dry sense of humor, and his customers loved it.

The coffeehouse was successful in the beginning.  Ike started off simple, with just regular and decaffeinated coffees, assorted teas, and a few baked goods that his wife, Annabelle whipped up in the small kitchen.  Customers frequented the coffeehouse from 6 am to about 10 am, then business died until 5 in the afternoon, when people began getting off work.  Rather than closing during the dead hours, Ike began serving sandwiches and soups for lunch, and he added a fountain soda machine to sell

Cokes, Diet Cokes, and Sprites.  With the new lunch options, the coffeehouse became busy all day.  Ike had to hire additional help to run the register and serve the drinks.  When he could, he liked to walk around the shop and talk to people, most of whom he knew.  He always made sure the customers were happy, and his warmth and regard for the customers made Ike and his family popular in the village.  Sam grew up in the village and in the coffeehouse.  He would get up early in the morning and help set up the shop before school started.  The school bus would pick him up right from the coffeehouse and drop him off in the afternoon.  Sam would do his homework at one of the tables and have a snack.  The Kellers would leave around 6 pm and go home for dinner, leaving the servers in charge of the store until closing time.  Ike would go back around 9 pm and help close down and run the till.  This went on for 27 years.

In February 2004, Annabelle went to the hospital for back surgery.  The night before surgery, Annabelle had a heart attack and went into a coma.  She had another heart attack the following morning and passed away.  The coffeehouse closed for a couple of days so that Ike and Sam could get everything in order and make all necessary arrangements.  Everyone in the village knew Annabelle, and there was a large turnout for her service.  Per village laws, there were no longer any funerals in the village due to occasional flooding.  The village had their own annual Memorial Day remembrances.

Ike continued to run the coffeehouse, but his heart was no longer in it.  Every morning he would look in the kitchen and expect to see Annabelle in there, making pound cakes, breads, and cookies.  Rather than hiring a baker, Ike began purchasing baked goods from the pie shop down the street, Miss American Pie.  It worked out for both businesses.  If people wanted a slice of pie with coffee, they would go to The Periodic Coffee House.  If they wanted a whole pie, they would go to Miss American.

Sam quit his job as an accountant so he could help run the coffeehouse.  He had been taking care of the books for years, so he knew the business well.  What he didn't know, Ike taught him.  Ike spent more and more time by himself at home, and Sam took on more and more responsibility.  Sam wanted to start open mic nights, poetry readings, and acoustic performances.  Ike didn't care what Sam did.  Sam also applied for an alcohol license so the coffeehouse could serve beer on the weekends.  If Ike disapproved, he never said.  Sam added a walk-in cooler for the kegs and began selling a few varieties of draft beer.  He also had the idea to start serving specialty coffees, lattes, and mochas.  This would help modernize the coffeehouse and bring it into the 21st century.

The coffeehouse continued to do good business, and the weekend beer sales were a success.  As Annabelle and Sam had done before, now Sam brought in his wife, Kaitlyn, and 8-year-old daughter, Laurel, into the business.  Just as Sam had done as a kid, Laurel helped set up in the morning and would help serve coffee in the afternoons.  The customers loved her and tipped her generously.

The river was frequented by waterfowl.  Ducks of several varieties and geese frequented the village, and the village had adopted them.  Many residents took time to sit on benches by the river and feed the birds bread or bird seed.  The Kellers did this as well, as their home was right on the river and the birds were typically in their yard.

One duck in particular, a mallard, followed the Kellers back to the coffeehouse one evening.  The duck had been in some sort of accident and had lost part of its upper bill.  Laurel had named him Gutterball, and he was her favorite.  He was the only one of the birds that would take bread from her hand, and he would let her pet his back.  As the Kellers went inside the coffeehouse, Gutterball stood at the door and quacked incessantly.  When Laurel would go to the door, he would run around in circles, but he would begin quacking again when she walked away.  Knowing the Health Department would frown on a duck in the coffeehouse, Sam tried to shoo the bird away.  Gutterball took a couple of steps back but would not leave.  When Sam went back inside, the duck returned and quacked some more.  Sam went out the back door and set up a box with an old blanket, then went back inside.  He and Laurel went back out the front door, past Gutterball, and around the building.  Looking back, Sam could see the duck following them.  As they reached the back of the building, Laurel knelt down and pointed to the box.  There was a small bowl filled with water and another bowl with bread.  Gutterball walked over, nabbed a piece of bread and took a drink from the water bowl.  Then he waddled into the box, sat down, and closed his eyes.  Sam and Laurel walked back through the back door.  Gutterball stayed in the box, sleeping.

After a few months, Ike stopped coming to the coffeehouse altogether.  He would stay up all night and sleep most of the day.  He found it hard to sleep at night and in their bed.  Most of the time he would sleep on the couch or in his recliner.  Sam would stop by just about every day to check in on him and make sure he had dinner.  On a cold night in November, almost 8 months to the day that Annabelle had died, Ike didn't answer the door.  Sam tried his key, but the chain was latched on the door, and he couldn't get in.  Panicking, Sam called his father's phone.  He could hear it ring in the house, but no one answered.  Sam called 911, and a fire truck was first on the scene.  After checking all the doors and windows, they opted to cut the chain.  A fireman entered the house while another held Sam back.  A minute later, the fireman returned.  "I'm sorry," he said, with his head bowed.  Ike had suffered a massive heart attack while sitting in his recliner watching television.  His head hung to one side and his hand draped over the arm of the chair.  The remote control lay on the floor.  A Golden Girls rerun was on.

Sam was devastated.  He felt lost and didn't know what to do, so he tried to focus on the coffeehouse.  He was trying different promotions, having specials such as if your name started with the same letter as a certain element on the periodic table, you would get a free cup of coffee.  He was booking more acoustic acts, now during the week instead of just the weekends, and he was serving beer during the week as well.  For a while the busyness sated him, but inside of him was a hole.  Even spending time with Kaitlyn and Laurel didn't help.  He knew he should probably talk to someone, but the doctor visits were too costly, and he was a fairly private person.

One night he took a long drive.  He planned to kill himself. He would just go off in the woods and shoot himself, but he couldn't bring himself to do it.  He couldn't do that to his family. He never told anyone what he had planned to do, and he never told anyone why he didn't do it.  It was one of the things he kept to himself, but the next day he was back to his old self.  He had a new outlook on life, and he actually smiled for the first time in months.

The next few years had been pretty good.  His relationship with Kaitlyn had gotten even stronger.  Laurel was growing and had entered high school.  She was a straight-A student and a scholar athlete in tennis and swimming.  Kaitlyn and Sam had another child, a boy.  They had named him Noah Isaac.  Isaac had been his father's name, but everyone called him Ike.

The energy plant upriver had closed down, taking a lot of jobs and tax dollars away from the village.  The village increased local taxes to make up for the shortage, but people began moving away.  Miss American Pies closed down shortly thereafter.  It wasn't long before A Portal Through Pages, the used book store, also closed. Lucky's Bar stayed open, though. People were now drinking more than ever. There were rumors that an investment group was beginning to buy up property in the area. It turned out to be true. No one knew what they were up to, but they bought several houses that were for sale in the village, then they bought the buildings along River Road that had contained the pie shop and the used book store. As more and more people moved out, this company came in and made offers on the houses. Generous offers. Landlords increased rent so that their tenants could no longer afford the housing, then they sold to the investment group. Pretty soon, there wasn't much left. There was no one to buy coffee anymore. The elderly died or moved into nursing homes. No one moved in. Eventually the offers came to Lucky's Bar and to The Periodic Coffee House. John Fenwick signed his name on the contract and sold the bar. Sam looked the offer over a few times and after looking at his books, realized he had no choice. He signed, too.

The investment company was a dummy company for a major golf magnate. They were expanding their holdings and looked to put a championship-caliber golf course in this area, right along the river. Without the homes and the businesses, this would be the perfect location, so long as they built up the course so that it was higher up, as the river was prone to flooding. They would demolish all the buildings, bulldoze all the roads, build up the land, plant grass, and ship in trees. Big, beautiful pine and magnolia trees, and lots of azalea bushes. It would be easy to ship the trees up the river, right to the course. The area that had been a river town for more than 200 years would be green once again. The riverboats would still roll down the river, but they would no longer stop in Nevileville.

Sam thought about all this as he drank his latte. It no

longer warmed his belly.  In fact, he thought that maybe he no longer liked coffee.  He poured the rest down the drain, washed and dried his mug, and placed it in a box filled with other mugs and utensils.  He walked to the door and turned the sign to CLOSED for the last time.  He switched off the light, walked out the door, and locked it behind him.

As he walked down River Road towards his house, he sighed as he looked at all the dark businesses and houses.  There was a quacking behind him, and he turned to see Gutterball waddling towards him.  He smiled and waited for the mallard to catch up, then Sam and the duck continued their walk home.

# The Firecracker Bunch

## <u>1</u>

My grandson, Nate, came over to "visit" me this morning. I say "visit" because most of the time he just sits around on his phone, texting, playing games, or on that Facebook or Twitter, or some other nonsense. I think most of the time he comes around just to get away from his folks, and that's ok. I love having him here, whatever the reason. Today was a nice summer day, though. It was hot, I know, but a 13-year-old boy should be outside in the sun, not hunkered down on the couch with an old man like me. We took a little walk down to The Periodic Coffee House, where I bought him a lemonade and a slice of apple pie. I got myself a cup of coffee and had a slice of pie too.

"Nate, did I ever tell you about The Firecracker Bunch?"

He looked up from his phone, briefly. "No, sir," he said.

Well, at least he had manners. "Put your phone down for a few minutes and let me tell you a story. It's all true, I promise, and I think you'll be interested."

Nate put his phone on the table, reluctantly, and looked at me. "Ok," he said.

"Alright, then," I started.

## <u>2</u>

The 4th of July 1966 was when we all got our nicknames. I

know it was 1966 because that was the year that Adam West became Batman.  Star Trek started later that year, too, and we were all out of the hospital by then.  Johnny Murphy became "Stubby," Hilda Benedict became "Holey Hilda" (we also called her 3-hole, but never to her face), Stanley Forster became "The Flash," my little brother Kenny became "Mittens," and I became known as "One-Eyed Jack."  That day started out fun and ended horribly, but at least we managed to get out of Vietnam because of it.  Except for Flash.

All this came to mind because of the letter I got in the mail.  It was from Stubby and was postmarked 5 days prior.  The handwriting was faint and hardly legible.  He was old, and you could tell his hand was shaking when he wrote it.  The letter read:

Hey, One-Eyed, you old bastard!  I just wanted to write to you and say goodbye.  I was diagnosed with lung cancer a year ago, and it's just about got me.  All those damned cigars.  You told me!  I'd call, but I can't talk without having a coughing spell.  Just as well.  It's easier this way.  We had some good times, huh?  A bunch of dumb kids we were!  I've missed you, Flash, Holey, and Mittens.  Guess it's just going be you now.  Take care, you coot!  See you at the Pearly Gates, and if I don't, well, then I guess I'll be looking up at you from Hell, shaking my fist at you.  You'll always be the brother I never had.

Sincerely,

*Stubby*

Well, damn, I thought.  I laid the letter on the counter and wiped my eyes.  I didn't want this to be the end of it, and I didn't know just how long Stubby had left.  I went into the kitchen and pulled out my address book from the junk drawer.  I hadn't opened the book in a long time; there weren't many people left I wanted to talk to anymore.  As I was thumbing through the pages, I passed by Benedict, Hilda.  There was a line through her contact information.  I came to the "F's."  Another line through Flash Forster.  I passed the "G's".  Garber, Kenny, my little brother.  Lined out.  I finally came to the middle of the alphabet, to the "M's" and to Stubby Murphy.

As I reached for the cordless phone, it began to ring, startling me.  I answer on the second ring.

"Hello," I said, my voice cracking.

"Mr. Garber?" a female voice asked.

"Yes, that's me," I replied.

"Hello, sir.  My name is Cindy Mahler.  Johnny Murphy is my father."

"Oh, hello, Cindy," I answered.  "I just got Stubby's letter today, and I was about to call him."

"I'm sorry, Mr. Garber.  My father passed away yesterday afternoon.  I thought you should know."

"Oh, God," I whispered.  "I'm so sorry," I said, wiping my eyes again.  "Were you with him?"

"Thank you, Mr. Garber.  Yes, I was with him when he passed.  I was holding his hand.  He was resting and didn't suffer at the end."

She seemed to be taking all this in stride, but I guessed she'd had a day to process it.  "I'm sure you took good care of him.  He always spoke highly of you.  I know he was proud of you."

I heard a little hitch in her voice.  "Thank you, Mr. Garber.

That means a lot.  You were like a brother to him.  The notice is in the newspaper.  My dad didn't want a big funeral.  The service will be Thursday at 9 am at the funeral home.  You know where it's at, right?"

"Yes, I do," I said, though I hadn't set foot in that building since Hilda passed, almost 20 years ago.  "I'll be there."

"Thank you, Mr. Garber."

"Thank you for calling, Cindy," I said as I hung up the phone.

I went to the bathroom, relieved myself, and washed my hands and face.  I walked into my home office and sat down at my desk.  My laptop was already open, so I Googled Stubby's name and the word "obituary," and the search came up with the link for the Clayton Herald's newspaper's website.  Stubby had moved to Clayton about 30 minutes outside of Nevileville, after college.  I clicked on the link and saw a picture of my best friend.

Tuesday, July 2

Jonathan Francis "Stubby" Murphy

Jonathan Francis Murphy, 68, entered into rest Monday, July 1, 2018 at his residence.  He was the son of the late Herschel Murphy and Vernice Chambliss Murphy.  He was preceded in death by his wife, the late Hilda Benedict Murphy.  He leaves behind a daughter, Cynthia Mahler, a son-in-law, Phillip Mahler, and twin granddaughters Terry Mahler and Claudia Mahler.

Born in Nevileville on February 19, 1950, Murphy, known as "Stubby" to his friends, was an avid golfer and fan of baseball and college football.  He received his undergraduate degree in Mortuary Science in 1973 and helped his father operate Murphy Family Funeral Home in Clayton.  Stubby was nationally renowned for his mastery of cosmetic arts, being able to perform facial and anatomical recreations in order to allow many of the departed to have open-casket funerals.  His work was in high demand, taking him across the country to do consulting and reconstruction work at several mortuaries and military installations.  He was a member of St. Bernadette's Catholic Church and was a member of several civic organizations in the Clayton area.

A devoted husband and loving father, and grandfather, Stubby Murphy will be greatly missed.  A private ceremony will be held at Murphy's Funeral Home on Thursday, July 4 at 9 am. A graveside service at Meadowlawn Cemetery will follow.  In lieu of flowers, the family asks that donations be made to the American Cancer Society.

Stubby had been my best friend growing up, but I hadn't seen him in about 12 years.  As kids, we were inseparable, the five of us, but Stubby and I were closer than even me and Mittens.  The only thing that ever got between me and Stubby was Hilda, and even that didn't last long.  I'm digressing a bit, so I guess I should just start at the beginning.

**<u>3</u>**

I was born and raised here in Nevileville.  Back in the late

1800s, it was a booming little river town filled with hotels, taverns, and even an opera house.  This was a big hub for the riverboats.  My daddy worked in a textile mill that made sheets, blankets, towels, and whatnot.  My mom worked the soda fountain at a pharmacy.  I know you might not know what a soda fountain was, so let me explain a little.  A lot of stores back then, places like Woolworth's Sky City, and H.L. Green's, as well as pharmacies, or drug stores, would have a little dining area.  It was mostly a counter and maybe a couple of tables, but most folks sat at the counter.  There would be a grill with a fry cook who would make hamburgers, footlong hot dogs, BLTs, and French fries.  The specialty, however, was always the root beer floats or milk shakes.  The food was much better than anything you could get at one of those fast-food places today.  That shit'll kill you.

My parents met in high school.  My dad dropped out after 10th grade so he could go to work and help out at home.  My mom was a year younger, and she graduated three years later.  This was in 1949.  They were married two weeks later, and I came along 6 months after that.  I know what you're thinking, and you're right.  That's all I'll say about that.  My brother Kenny was born two years later, in 1952.  Times were tough, and money was scarce.  A lot of times we would wear hand-me-downs from some cousins or neighbors.  Back then, neighbors knew each other.  Neighbors visited each other, sat a spell, and had actual conversations.  Neighbors watched out for each other's' kids.  If you did something wrong in the neighborhood, you might get your ass spanked three or four times before you even got home, and when you did get home, daddy would make you go outside and break off a switch from a bush, and you'd get your ass beat some more.  No, it wasn't child abuse.  It toughened you up and made you respect your parents and authority.

We all lived in the same neighborhood, me and my brother,

Stubby, Hilda, and Flash.  Stubby lived next door, Flash lived across the street, three houses down, and Hilda lived around the corner on the next street.  There were several other neighborhood kids, too, but the five of us palled around more than any of the others.  Hilda was kind of a tomboy back then, so she kept up with us.  We would play baseball, wrestle, go fishing or swimming at the aqueduct, which we called the "Achy Docks."  Every now and again we'd play school a little, with Hilda as the teacher, or just sit around under a shade tree and drink some of Stubby's mother's lemonade.  Sometimes we might have a tea party or play dolls with Hilda, just because she always did what we wanted to do, but we'd always do that stuff indoors, where other folks wouldn't see us.

One thing we always would do was pull pranks on each other.  They were always harmless pranks, but sometimes we would get in trouble if the prank ended up on one of our parents instead of on us.  We would hide and scare each other, have fake snakes, pour salt in the sugar bowl or sugar in the salt shaker, put plastic wrap under the toilet seat so that when you went, it would splash back up on, things like that.  Pretty harmless, like I said.

In the summer of 1966, Stubby, Hilda, and I were 16.  Flash would turn 16 in October, and my brother was 14.   I was working at a gas station pumping gas and checking oil, Hilda was working at the soda fountain with my mom, and Stubby was working for his old man at the funeral home, mostly cleaning the floors and learning the family trade.  We had a little spending money.  Every year around the 4th of July, we would get some fireworks.  We couldn't get them here, so we would have to go over into Kentucky.  None of us could drive yet, so we would walk on the railroad tracks that crossed the Ohio River.  It wasn't that far, but if a train came, you had nowhere to go but down!  It was stupid, yes, but we didn't think like that then.  The fireworks stand was just on the other side of the river, across the state line, and the tracks were the fastest and easiest way for us to get those fireworks.

Big Mike's Fireworks was nothing special; it was really just a wooden stand.  It was open only for about three weeks a year, just before the 4th.  We weren't really looking for anything fancy, just some firecrackers, bottle rockets, and some sparklers for Kenny.  He wasn't much into fireworks.  We paid, and Big Mike put the fireworks in a brown bag.

"You kids going back across the river?" he asked.

"Yes, sir," Flash answered.

"Just be careful that the cops don't see you with 'em.  You know they're illegal over there."

"Yes, sir," I said.  "We'll be careful."

"And make sure it's not dry where you light them.  We've been in a dry spell for a coupla weeks."

"We will, thanks," Hilda said sweetly.

The sweetness of her voice kinda ticked me off, I'm ashamed to say.  We had all been great friends, and none of us had thought about Hilda as a girl.  That is, until she turned 14 and started to develop.  Then we started to look at her a little differently, but we were all too scared to say or do anything, except for good old Johnny, my best friend.  Earlier that spring I had caught them kissing down by the Achy Docks when none of the rest of us were around.  I didn't say anything, I just turned and ran home.  I hadn't realized until then that I loved Hilda.  I never told her though.  She and Johnny dated through high school and then got married after college.  I was the best man at their wedding. There were two pranks that day.  The second was when Hilda smashed a piece of wedding cake into Stubby's face, but that was typical of wedding receptions.  The first and biggest one was that Stubby had married the woman I secretly loved.  He loved her, too, and he took a shot, whereas I did nothing.  I only had myself to blame.  That didn't mean that I had to like it.

Anyway, we crossed back across the river.  It was a hot day.  We walked a couple of miles back to the Achy Docks and the canal.  We got over by the dam, sat on the grass and divided our fireworks.  We each got a few firecrackers and bottle rockets, except for Kenny, who got his sparklers.  We spread out a little bit along the canal because we didn't want to be too close to each other.  We started out just throwing firecrackers or shooting bottle rockets at signs or at turtles who were sunning on logs.  We never intended on getting into a war, but that's what happened.

<u>4</u>

Dipshit Stanley started it all, throwing a firecracker that exploded a couple of feet in front of Hilda.  She jumped back and fell onto her rear end.  That pissed off Johnny, who lit a bottle rocket and aimed it at Stanley, who turned to run.  He was slow as molasses, and the bottle rocket hit him square in the back.  He yelped, but he wasn't really hurt.  I was laughing at him, so hard I nearly fell over.  "Way to get away, Flash," I said, chuckling.  That's how he got the nickname, and it stuck.

"What are you laughing at?" Flash asked, lighting a bottle rocket.  The rocket flew at me, and I ducked.  The rocket flew past me and landed right by Hilda's behind.  It was the damndest thing.  The bottle rocket exploded right there at her left butt cheek, burning a hole through her shorts and panties.  She had a quarter-sized burn mark on her butt, so she said, but I never saw it.  That's how she ended up with the name "Holey Hilda."

Hilda was crying, but she was pissed.  So was Johnny.  They were both lighting firecracker after firecracker, tossing them at Flash.  He kept running, but his slow ass kept getting hit.  As Johnny was lighting one firecracker in particular the damned thing went off in his hand.  It had a short fuse.  The explosion took off the tip of Johnny's middle finger, just past the nail.  He didn't even realize it at the time, but I saw it happen.  The tip of his finger flew off and landed in the canal, probably to be eaten by a catfish.  That's how he got the name "Stubby."  I was yelling at Johnny to stop, Hilda was crying, Johnny was cursing, and Flash was running.  Kenny was standing off to the side, holding his sparklers.  Johnny lit one final bottle rocket, aiming it at Flash.  As he did, Flash started running towards me.  I could see it all in slow motion, which was Flash's normal speed.  Johnny's hand changed direction, and the bottle rocket flew.  Flash got a sudden burst of real speed and ran past me.  The bottle rocket flew towards me, and there was nothing I could do but yell, oh, sh.."  I didn't even finish my curse before the rocket hit me square in the right eye.  Fortunately, the rocket fell to one side, and I fell to the other.  It exploded just before it hit the ground.  If it had exploded when it hit my eye, I would have been blinded.  As it was, I just lost vision in that eye for a few days while it was sore and swollen.  I had to wear a patch during that time, which is why they started calling me "One-Eyed Jack."  Everything got quiet then.  That's when we heard my brother Kenny screaming.  In all the excitement, he had forgotten he was holding the sparklers.  He had them all lit, and they burned down and seared both of his hands.

We all raced home as fast as we could, which was still about a mile from the canal.  Pretty soon we were all at the

University Hospital emergency room with our parents.  Hilda had a burn on her butt cheek, but it wasn't bad.  Flash wasn't hurt too badly either; he just had a couple of burn marks and several bruises on his back and stomach.  Stubby's finger was stitched up and bandaged.  From then on, it was pretty funny when he'd shoot us the bird.  My eye was bandaged and then patched.  I would regain sight in it about 4 days later.  Both of Kenny's hands had second-degree burns on them, all over the palms.  They put a salve on his bands, bandaged them, and then had him wear protective gloves for a couple of weeks.  This is how he became known as Mittens.  It was probably worse on him than anyone else because he couldn't do much with his hands, at least for the first couple of days.  Mom had to feed him and bathe him.  I think the bathing was probably the worst for him because he was 14 and was embarrassed.  Mom let him wear a bathing suit in the bath tub.

Our parents weren't happy about that, not at all.  We all got our butts spanked, except for Holey Hilda, and we were grounded for the rest of the summer.  All of our parents knew we were pretty good kids, just a little mischievous.  When we started back to school in the middle of August, we were the stars of the school, at least for the first week.  Everyone had heard about our fireworks battle, even though it had not gotten into the newspaper.  The police had been notified, and we had gotten a talking to, but they were afraid if it was publicized there might be other firecracker wars.

Over the next two years at school, we were all inseparable, and we continued to play jokes on one another.  Us boys had what we called the "Shot to the Ribs Club."  If we saw one another in the hallway at school, we would sneak up and try to punch the other in the ribs.  Not too hard, but enough to give you a good jolt and make you drop your books or whatever.  Especially if you were talking to a girl at the time.  We also set loose a bunch of crickets in the girls' bathroom one time.  That was pretty funny!  You should have seen them run out of there!  There was always the prank phone call, too.  We would call our parents or a store and ask things like, "Is your refrigerator running?  Yes, well you better go catch it!" or "Do you have Prince Albert in a can?  Well, you better let him out before he dies."  You know, stupid stuff like that, but it was hilarious at the time.  Hilda was getting more girly and didn't prank as much or do tomboy stuff with us much anymore.  When she wasn't with Stubby, she was hanging out with her cheerleader friends.

Stubby and I were on the high school football team.  He had been a quarterback before the finger incident.  Now he played linebacker.  I was a fullback.  We had some pretty decent teams, but nothing spectacular, and we weren't college football prospects.  Flash was on the debate team.  Sometimes we would heckle him during a debate or, if we could get hold of his note cards, would change them or put them out of order.  Again, stupid pranks.  He would always get us back though, like putting hot sauce in our jock straps or something like that.

After high school, Stubby started mortuary school, and Hilda took stenography classes.  She became a court reporter.  Stubby's father had moved the family business to Clayton, and Stubby and Hilda moved there when they got married.  Stubby continued on with the family business and became very successful.  As I mentioned earlier, he was an artist when it came to facial reconstruction.  He did work in D.C., California, Florida, Ft. Bragg, Charleston, and a host of other places.  He had to hire additional help at the funeral home because he was in such demand and travelling so much.  With Vietnam going on, there were a lot of soldiers that came home, and Stubby worked with a lot of ones that otherwise would have been closed caskets.  Stubby and Hilda had the one daughter, Cindy, the one who called me.  Cindy had twin daughters, who are 10.  Hilda was diagnosed with breast cancer in 1997.  By the time it was caught, it was too late.  She passed away 6 months later.  She was just 47.  I was there for Stubby.  Life had moved us apart, but we were still like brothers and would talk on the phone from time to time.  Three or four times a year we would get together and have lunch or double date with our wives.  After Hilda died, he kind of shut himself off, and I didn't hear from him much.  We would still call each other every now and then, but the last time I saw him was at a golf outing in 2005.

I went to school at the University of Cincinnati.  Ironically, I became an ophthalmologist.  One of my first patients, Ingrid Taylor, ended up becoming my wife, your.  She was a little forward and actually asked me out.  She was beautiful and smart, so of course I said yes.  After dating for two years, we were married in 1978.  Our son Elijah was born in 1980.  We had another son, Jack Jr., who was born in 1983.  He was premature and died two weeks later.  The loss really took its toll on Ingrid.  She became very depressed and starting drinking.  She was seeing a therapist for depression was put on medication.  In 1985 she overdosed on antidepressants, leaving me a widower with a 5-year-old son.  It was tough, but we made it work.  Most of the time during the summers, Elijah, your dad, would come with me to work, and he would play or read in my office most of the day.  As you know, he later became an ophthalmologist and took over my practice.

Flash was set on going to Ohio State to become a mechanical engineer, but war called.  He was drafted into the Army and was sent to Vietnam after basic training.  He was there three days before stepping on a land mine.  Even Stubby couldn't fix that.  Flash's parents were devastated and ended up moving out of the area shortly after that.  Flash was buried at Arlington, and his father took a job in that area so they could be near him.

My brother graduated from high school in 1972 and joined the Air Force.  His hands had obviously gotten better by then.  After serving for four years, Mittens took a job with American Airlines as a commercial pilot.  In 1981 he was in Athens, Greece on vacation.  He was mugged late at night and attempted to fight off the thief.  The robber stabbed him and left him lying in the street.  Mittens was found twenty minutes later and taken to a hospital, but he had lost too much blood.  He had just turned 27 and had never been married.

So that's the story of the Firecracker Bunch, as the neighborhood started calling us after the incident.  It was kind of a sore subject at first, since we were all recovering and all grounded, but eventually it became funny and cool.  As traumatizing as it could have been, that became one of the best memories of our lives.

<u>5</u>

Before I went to bed on July 3, I knelt by my bed and prayed.  I asked the Lord to grant Stubby's family the strength to get through the next day and the weeks and months ahead.  I also prayed for Stubby's soul, and I knew he was at peace, again with his Hilda.

With a heavy heart I woke up early the next morning.  I wasn't very hungry, but I forced myself to eat a piece of toast with butter and drank of glass of orange juice.  I showered and shaved then dressed in my gray suit that I had set out the night before.  At

8:10, I left the house, picking up the brown paper bag off the counter as I left the kitchen.  It would take almost half an hour to get to the funeral home in Clayton.

<u>6</u>

The drive was uneventful.  It had been a while since I had been to Clayton, and the area had grown and developed.  There was a few more fast-food joints and motels just off 275 than I remembered.  The funeral home was about 5 miles down the road, and I got there about a quarter to 9.

There were only about a dozen people in the funeral home when I arrived, far less than I expected, but then Cindy said it was a private funeral and Stubby didn't want a big to do.  There were a few folks standing around the coffin, so I waited by the door a few moments.  Cindy came up to me and said hello.  She introduced me to her husband.  Her daughters were not there.

"I didn't want them to see their grandpa like this," she said. "They're with a babysitter."

"I understand," I said.  "I don't want to see him like this either."

As the area around the coffin emptied, I made my way up to see Stubby.  He looked good.  Real good.  Peaceful.  I reached into the bag in my coat pocket and pulled out a big wad of firecrackers.  I had fashioned some extra-long fuses onto them and bound them together.  When I knew nobody was looking, I lit one of the fuses and placed the whole bunch as far down the casket as I could, and then I moved away.  I knew I had a few seconds.

It actually took longer than I expected.  At first, I thought maybe I had a dud or that the fuse had been snuffed out.  Just as the priest signaled for us to make our way into the chapel, a whirr like a wet fart came from the casket.  Everyone turned around just in time to see the bottom door of the casket blow off its hinges in a big explosion.  The casket teetered off its gurney and toppled to the floor.  Stubby rolled out of the overturned casket.  Well, at least his torso did, for that's all there was.  The dozen or so people gasped, and somebody, I think it was Cindy's husband, but it could have been the priest, exclaimed, "Holy Shit!"

I laughed and yelled, "Not holy shit, Holey Hilda!  That's for her and for my eye, you crotchety old son of a bitch!"

Everyone turned and looked at me in shock but then turned back to Stubby, whose suit jacket was now on fire.  I yelled for someone to get a fire extinguisher, but it was too late; Stubby's face had started to melt!  What hair he had left burned away, his cheeks withered and melted, and his eyeballs rolled right out of his head!  Nobody rushed to put him out, so I started forward, but a gentle hand held me back.  It was Cindy.  She was smiling.

All of a sudden there was raucous laughter, followed by a hacking cough.  I turned to the door of the parlor, and there was Stubby, standing there nearly doubled over from laughing so hard.

"What in the hell, Stubby?" I asked.

Stubby finally stopped coughing, laughed again, and wheezed," I got you, you one-eyed asshole!" "Ha ha ha!  You thought you were getting one over on me, but I've been planning this for two years!"

I looked around.  It all made sense now.  That's why this

was a private funeral, held at the funeral home and not at St. Bernadette's. These were all Stubby's family and his daughter's friends. They were all in on it!

"But you were there," I said, pointing to the molten remains on the now singed carpet.

"Wax, jackass," he exclaimed. "You know I'm the best mortician and reconstructionist in the country. I made a mold of myself out of wax. Took me three months to get it just right. I even used some of my real hair!"

I didn't know whether to hug him or beat the hell out of him. We were old, and he was my best friend, so I held out my hand. We shook hands and then embraced. We were both crying.

"I knew you loved Hilda and you were bitter over it, but you never said anything," Stubby said.

"No, I didn't. I never told her, and you won her fair and square."

"She wasn't a prize to be won, Jack," he said.

"Yes, she was," I said, "and so are you," I stated, punching him in the ribs.

Stubby doubled over again as his son-in-law stepped forward. Stubby held up his hand, and Phillip stopped. "Damned shot to the ribs club," Stubby said hoarsely and laughed. Then he stood up and said, "all this dying's made me hungry. Let's go eat!"

"What about all this?" I asked him, motioning towards the overturned casket and the blob on the floor.

"I pay people to clean," he said. "Let's eat."

We all went down the road to Golden Corral and had a buffet lunch.  Stubby and I told stories about our childhood.  We laughed and we cried, and we laughed some more.

## 7

Stubby passed away three months later.  He really did have lung cancer.  He set the whole prank up so that we could have fun one more time before he passed.  I saw him more those last three months than I had in the past fifteen years.  I was with him in the hospital when he passed away.  This was just last year.  He was my best friend and my brother.  We let too much time go by without seeing or talking to each other, and I can never get that time back.  I'm the only one of the Firecracker Bunch left now, and all I have are memories.

So that's my story, kid.  I wanted to share that with you because we are never promised tomorrow.  I love you, and I love your daddy.  He's a good man, but he's way too serious.  It's just his nature, but he needs to loosen up a little.  And you, grandson, you need to have some fun, too.  You have some friends in the neighborhood, don'tcha?"  He looked at me and nodded.  "Here, take this bag then."

"What's in it, Grandpa?" my 13-year-old grandson asked.

"What do you think?  Open it up."

Nate opened the bag, and his eyes grew wide.  "Fireworks!" he shouted.

"Indeed," I told him.  "Go make some memories.  Start your own Firecracker Bunch.  Just be careful, ok?"

Nate gave me a great big hug, told me he loved me and to be careful, and ran out the door with the bag.  I paid the waitress and walked back to the house.  That night we ended up in the emergency room, but that's a different story, and not mine to tell.

# **Memorial Day**

Kyle Hutchinson, "Hutch" to his friends, relocated his family from Georgia to Ohio.  His company, one of the big ones, had corporate headquarters in Cincinnati, and after years of working in manufacturing facilities, his technical mastery had been rewarded with a corporate position.  He had worked in Industrial Hygiene and Safety for the last twelve years, had earned a graduate degree, and his professional certifications added letters to the end of his name.

When the moving van rolled into the tiny river village of Nevileville, population 916 (based on the 2010 census), those in town turned and stared.  Kyle later found out that the town did not get many "newbies," as they would be called.  The house they bought wasn't even listed by a real estate firm; one of his new colleagues had inherited the property from an uncle who had recently passed.  Kyle had gotten to take a look at the property when he travelled for his relocation house-hunting trip.

The house was at the far end of the town green, a corner

lot, and cater-cornered from the library and post office.  The house had been built in 1872 but didn't look a day over 100 years old.  It needed a little fixing up, mostly some painting and a new roof, but it had good bones.  It was a two-story Victorian and had a fully finished basement as well.  There was a white picket fence in the front yard along the sidewalk, and the backyard had a vinyl privacy fence that surrounded its 0.5 acres.

There was a house next door to the Hutchinson's, another two-story Victorian that was painted sky blue.  There were no cars in the driveway, but the lawn was manicured, so Kyle assumed they had neighbors.

The neighbors turned out to be George and Eileen Somerset.  They had been out shopping at the IGA when the moving van arrived.  Kyle raised a hand in hello when he saw the Explorer pull into the driveway next door.  George returned a two-finger salute.  They got out of the SUV and walked over to meet the new neighbors.

The Somersets seemed friendly enough, but George

reminded Kyle of the germophobe in that crazy Stephen King movie *Creepshow*.  He had white hair that was just a bit too long, and it was unkempt, sort of like Albert Einstein.  Kyle figured that the Somersets were in the mid-60s.

Kyle introduced the couple to his wife, Margot, and their children, Edie, who was 11, and Barry, who had just turned 7.  After a short visit, the Somersets remembered their groceries.  "Can't let the ice cream melt," said George.  "Wouldn't want Rocky Road syrup," he said with a chuckle.  Hutch returned the laugh.  "We'll have to have you over for dinner once we get settled, he said."  "We'll bring the wine," George answered, and the Somersets moved back to the SUV.

The summer was rather uneventful.  The Hutchinsons settled in and began exploring their new area, venturing out on day trips to the zoo, the museum, and even to Brown County and Serpent Mound, a Native American earthworks.  It was hot, but they were from Georgia, so they were kind of used to the heat.  There were cookouts with the Somersets.  Sometimes Margot and Eileen had a cup of coffee together in the morning, either in their own kitchens or sometimes down at The Periodic Coffee House in the village.  George and Hutch would sometimes have a beer on the porch in the evening.

When fall came around, the kids started school.  They adapted quickly and made friends.  Edie joined the girls' volleyball team and Barry played soccer.  They both made straight A's.  On Friday nights, the sleepy little village seemed to come alive for Nevileville high school football.  The games always started at 7 pm, but the town would have a parade where the football players and cheerleaders would drive through town (juniors and seniors in the own vehicle, freshmen and sophomores on the team bus) to the green, where there would be a pep rally.  After the pep rally, the villagers would caravan behind the team bus up to Fighting Otter Stadium (for home games) or to one of the opponent's fields, like Amelia, Loveland, or Anderson.  If the Otters won, the team would come back to the green and ring the large ceremonial bell, one time for every point they scored.  You could hear the ringing of the bell for miles!

On a cool Saturday night in October, George and Hutch

were sitting on the Somerset's front porch having a cold one.  The ladies were on the back porch talking while the kids played in the backyard with the Somerset's Jack Russell, Skippy.

As they watched a couple walking their dog on the village green, Hutch said, "Hey, George, I've been meaning to ask you something."

"Sure, go ahead," George replied.

"I've noticed something about the town."

"Have you?" George asked, raising an eyebrow.  "What's that?"

"Well, I know this is a small village, but I haven't seen any churches here.  Usually you find one on every street corner.  Edie's started asking about going to church, and I was trying to find one close by."

George let out an audible sigh.  "Well, folks 'round here are a thankful bunch, but we've kinda soured on organized religion over the years.  The closest church is up around Hamlet."

"Oh, well what do you do about weddings and funerals?" Hutch asked.

"Most weddings take place at the Town Hall, performed by the Justice of the Peace.  As for funerals, we don't have cemeteries in town due to flooding.  Had a problem some years ago.  Bodies washed up right out of the graves. Happened pretty frequently, so they all ended up getting moved. We have our own annual village ceremony each year now."

"I see," Hutch replied, but he didn't, not really.

Fall gave way to winter.  It was unseasonably warm that year.  Well, not warm, but not really cold, either.  Hutch didn't mind; he wasn't a fan of the cold.  He had bought a snow blower, but fortunately had not had to use it.  The bit of snow they had gotten had been manageable.  Edie and Barry continued in sports; Edie joined the swim team, and Barry donned a singlet and started wrestling.  They were both getting to be tall for their age and were good athletes.  They continued to be on the honor roll every 9 weeks, earning trips to the zoo and aquarium.

At Christmastime, the village decorated the green with twinkling lights.  There was a Santa on a sleigh drawn by 9 tiny reindeer, with Rudolph and his shiny nose at the head of the pack.  On Christmas Eve, Kyle and his family joined the Somersets down by the village gazebo, where the high school chorus was signing carols.  It seemed the entire village turned out for the affair, which included free hot chocolate and marshmallows that could be roasted over a fire pit that had been set up on the green.  The villagers sand along to "Silent Night," O, Christmas Tree," Frosty the Snow Man," and several other holiday favorites.  Margot took Kyle's hand, and he turned to look at her.

"I love it here," she whispered.

"I do, too," he replied and kissed her on the forehead.

Winter begat spring, the flowers began to grow, and so did the grass.  The Somersets had become more than neighbors, they were friends.  At some point every day, the families connected.  Margot and Eileen would have coffee and exchange recipes or hang laundry outside together on their clotheslines when there were no April showers.  Kyle and George would see each other outside after Kyle got off work.  There was grass to cut and hedges to trim, which always led to a beer or three on the porch.

At the end of May, the village put on their annual Memorial Day celebration.  The village was decked out in red, white, and blue.  The village parade that morning consisted of the typical motorcade with the mayor and his wife riding atop a convertible, the Shriners with their little go karts, Tina Richards, who was this year's reigning Miss Nevileville, several classic cars, local fire trucks, ambulances, and police vehicles, and a convertible carrying Vernon Allenson, the oldest living veteran from Nevileville, 94 years of age.  There were also cheerleaders and bands from the high and middle schools, several horses and riders, a group of alpacas from the alpaca farm, and even a contingency of pigs, oinking and hoofing it down Main Street with their owners on either side to keep them within the bounds of the road.  For the kids, and even some adults, this was the highlight of the parade.

As the parade ended, the villagers moved to the green for the annual Memorial Day lunch and remembrance ceremony.  The grills had been set up, white smoke was pouring out, and the aromas were heavenly. The village put on this shindig every year without cost to the villagers. There was food, food, and more food. The grill tops were covered with hamburgers, hot dogs, ribs, and sausages. The red and white-checkered tables were covered with corn on the cob, beans, both green and baked, salads of the garden, potato, and macaroni varieties, watermelon, jello, chocolate chip cookies, cakes and pies of all types, and popsicles. For drinks, there was bottled water, lemonade, and sweet tea. Friends, family, and neighbors loaded up plates and sat down at picnic tables to feast. The Hutchinsons and Somersets were at one long table, across from each other.

Kyle picked up a rib and began pulling the meat with his teeth. It was a little dry, but the rub on it had good flavor, a mix of sweet, smoky, and pepper. He reached for the bottle of barbecue sauce on the table and made eye contact with George, who was sitting across from him. Kyle smiled and nodded. George nodded back.

On stage, Terry Whiting, the village mayor, stepped up to

the podium and tapped the microphone.  Satisfied with the volume,

he began to speak.

"Residents of Nevileville, welcome to our town's 154th

annual Memorial Day Cookout and Day of Remembrance."  The

townspeople stopped eating long enough to applaud, whistle, and

give several hoots.  "Today," Whiting continued, "is the day of the

year in which we come together to honor not only the veterans who

have fought and died for our country, but also for our friends and

loved ones who have passed on this past year and have offered

themselves to us this day.  We give thanks to them and to our Lord

and Maker for providing us and for our blessings, health, and

community.  Our town registrar, Maya Langston, will now do the

honors and call out those that have passed"

The villagers cheered again, and Maya Langston stepped

up to the podium.  In a solemn voice, she called out, "Vera

Albemarle, 1929 to 2015."  Hutch did not notice.  Realization

began to set in, and he set down the rib.  "Offered?" he thought,

looking down at his plate.  He looked up again and across the

table.  George was watching him.  Kyle started to open his mouth, but George shook his head.  He lifted his hand and put a finger to his lips.  Then George pointed over to the restroom area.

"Joseph Ashworth, 1934-2016."

Kyle got Margot's attention.  "I'll be right back.  I have to go to the restroom."

"Are you okay?" she asked.  "You look a little flushed."

Kyle tried to smile.  "I'm okay.  Just the sun, I guess."

"Okay," she said and went back to her hamburger.  Edie and Barry were both eating hot dogs and laughing.  Barry was being Barry, making faces and being silly.

Kyle got up and started towards the restroom.  George was already there.  As Kyle walked across the lawn passed the picnic tables, he noticed several of the villagers staring at him, even Mayor Whiting.  As he got closer, George pushed open the door to the restroom and went inside.

It was cool inside.  The lights were on, but it was dim.  George stood by one of the restroom's two sinks.  He looked tired.

"I can tell that you know now," he said, matter-of-factly. "Before you say anything, let me explain."

Kyle started to open his mouth, but again George shook his head. "Let me explain," he said.

George stared past Kyle and began to speak. "The Village of Nevileville was established in in 1804, by Josiah Neville, who opened the Neville Mill, which processed cotton for use in clothing and linens. He also opened a dry goods store that stood where the Nevilleville Historical Society now stands. Anyway, the town started to grow and became pretty prosperous over the next decade, what with the river traffic and whatnot. The village had a couple of nice hotels on the river for when tourists came through, and there were several saloons and eating establishments. We even had an opera house, if you can believe that. Then in June of 1861, shortly after the start of the Civil War, a boat came up the river carrying a family of Negroes who were on the run from Georgia. They were slaves and were trying to get to the North so they could be free. The Reverend Claude Montgomery met the boat down at the docks where Albany Street is now. It was about one in the morning.  He had a wagon and got them all in.  There were five slaves in all.  Their name was Stone, taken after their master's surname.  No one ever learned their first names. "

George paused a moment, let out a sigh, and continued, "The Reverend started back to his house up the hill in the wagon, carrying his passengers.  Only problem was, Claude was seen. Virgil Sullivan, who ran the River Queen Saloon, was just locking up the bar when he saw the Negroes getting into the wagon, and he watched the Reverend drive the wagon up the hill.  There were several fellows in town that didn't take a liking to "the coloreds," as they were called, and Virgil was able to round up a lynch mob pretty quickly.  They walked up the hill with ropes and guns, and torches, right up to the Reverend's house.  Montgomery saw the torches and came outside to try to reason with the mob, but they took him and bound his arms.  Mrs. Montgomery, Abigail, was inside the house with the Negroes and her four-month-old son, Jasper.  She grabbed the Rev's shotgun and started shooting from the window.  Well, instead of returning fire, two of the men used their torches to set the porch on fire.  The wood wasn't treated, of course, like it is today, and that house went up quickly.  People in the village later said you could hear the screams coming from up the hill.  Every one of the Stones, along with Abigail and Jasper Montgomery, were killed in the blaze.  The Rev tried to break free to save his family, but one of the men hit him in the back of the head with his shotgun and knocked him cold.

With the deed done, the men carted the Rev back down to the village where they were planning to hang him.  When Reverend Claude came to, they hoisted him to his feet and placed the noose around his neck, which was attached to that big oak tree that still stands right out there on the edge of the village green.  Before they hung him, Billy Kenton, the sheriff and part of the lynch mob, asked him if he had any final words.  The Reverend looked around at each of them, with fury in his eyes, and said, 'May God damn you all to Hell for your actions against the innocent.  Damn you and damn this village.'

Sheriff Kenton looked at the Reverend, spat and replied, 'Weren't no innocents in that house or inside that rope.  You're the one who's damned, Reverend.  You and your family for trying to hide them coloreds.'  With that he signaled, and two of the men hoisted the rope.  They tied it off, as the Reverend's feet began to kick, trying to find purchase.  Soon his legs stopped flailing."

"That was the beginning of the problems," George stated.  The Ohio has had a history of flooding, but that summer and the next, were worse than ever.  In August 1861, a heavy storm came through, and it rained for three days.  The river rose, and before you knew it, the village started to flood.  Anything below the second floor of buildings was underwater.  People took to the streets in boats to get people out of houses.  The safest place was up the hill, but nobody wanted to go up there.  After about a week, the water receded, and people made repairs.  The next summer, June 1862, the town flooded again, this time worse than the year before.  About half of the town was destroyed and washed down river.  The cemetery was flooded, too.  Headstones were washed over, and many of the caskets started coming out of the ground.  The dead were floating down the street.  Loved ones tried to catch them before they floated on down the Ohio, but many were lost.  It was at that point that Richard Truman, who was mayor at the time, called a meeting of the townsfolk and asked for suggestions. It was brought up in that meeting that the problems had started after the lynching a year before. You have to remember that people were very superstitious back then, which I guess has carried on here now. Anyway, it was suggested that the town make an offering to the Lord and pray for forgiveness. They didn't want to rebury the dead because they were afraid this would happen again. They took what was left of the bodies, built a pyre, and basically cremated their dead. Much of the crops on the farms had been devastated by the flooding, and a lot of livestock had been washed away, too. Two days later, when Virgil, who ran the saloon, died suddenly of a heart attack, the mayor called another meeting to decide what they should do. Again, they didn't want to bury him, for fear that the river might end up washing him up again. And, being a tall and heavy man, it was a shame to waste so much meat, especially since they'd lost a large portion of their livestock. Obviously, one man couldn't feed a whole village, but it was enough to feed a large group. And you know what? The sun came out! People cheered and started the work of rebuilding again.

Over the course of the next couple of weeks, three more villagers died.  One fell from a ladder while trying to hammer a board back in place.  Another had a heat stroke and fell dead down on Main Street.  Then a farmer, John Barnes, died after getting kicked in the head by his horse when he was trying to reshoe him.  The townspeople got together and had a memorial service for the three that had died, and the Mayor also acknowledged the ones that had been buried in the cemetery that had risen and been cremated.  The meat was cooked, and the town ate.  This began the Memorial Day celebration.  We keep it to this day because, even though we're small, the town has been pretty well off.  There have been no major floods since then, although we have built a levee and moved the village to a little higher ground.  We have no funeral homes and no cemeteries, as you have seen; we have no need for them.  When someone dies, they go over to Al at the butcher shop, and he takes care of them.  What's left is cremated and released into the river.  Ashes to ashes, and all that.  We have no need of a church or a reverend, either.  This green is our church, and the Memorial Day celebration is our offering."

At this point, George stopped.  Kyle was staring at the man, almost in disbelief.  Finally, Kyle asked," After 154 years, how is it that nobody else knows about this?  You'd think the government, the news, or someone would pick up on it."

George smiled a tired smile at Kyle.  "Well, we've been fortunate, but we also look after our own and keep to ourselves.  There have been some questions, of course.  There have been a couple of reporters that have snooped around over the years, but we've taken care of them."  George did not elaborate.  "As for any other media, we run the county newspaper.  Any village obituaries are run in our own newspaper, but they never get published in the county's.  As for cemeteries, well, the village passed a law outlawing cemeteries because of the flooding.  So far as anyone knows, anyone who dies here gets cremated.  The state and federal government don't question that.  It's legal, so that's that.  As for outsiders, well, like I said, we keep to our own.  Most of the villagers are lifers; not too many people move out, and not too many move in.  Your family was a rare case.  You slipped through the cracks, so to speak.  That's why we've been watching you.

You didn't know it, but we were.  Now you're one of us, and folks like you.  But now you know our secret, and we can't let that secret out.  So, my question to you, Hutch, is, 'What are you going to do about it?'"

We went back to the green and sat down at the table.  Edie and Barry were both working on new hot dogs.  Margot smiled at Kyle and asked," Are you okay?  You were gone for a while."

Kyle smiled back and said, "Yes, I'm okay.  Stomach's just a little upset, but I'm okay.  How is your burger?"

"It's really good," she said.  "How are the ribs?"

Kyle looked up at the sky.  It was a warm, sunny day.  All blue without a cloud in the sky.  "They're a little dry, but tender," he replied as he picked up the rib.

# Black Birds in the Field

I don't know what kind of birds they were.  Hell, I ain't no bird scientist.  We didn't have Google back then, and we certainly didn't have no damned Alexa.  I know that red birds are cardinals, and I know what blue jays are.  I know robins and doves and owls and hawks and eagles, but I don't know what these birds were, and I didn't know why they were there neither.  I still don't know for sure, but I have my suspicions.

They were big and black with curved beaks.  They weren't crows or their cousin ravens.  Maybe they were turkey vultures.  I don't know.  Don't matter much, does it?  Most damned birds I've ever seen, by volume, I reckon.  More every day, at least for a while, and then they started tapering off.  I've seen flocks of birds take off, but they were usually smaller birds.  These birds were big, and they didn't take flight.  Those sons of you know what weren't scared of nothing.  Weren't scared of headlights or flashlights, car horns, or even an air horn that I blew one day.  I was testing them, you see?  Hell, I think they were testing me.  I even stopped the car and got out one morning and tried to walk up on them.  The way they all turned and glared at me pert near scared the bejesus out of me.  I certainly got back into my truck faster than I got out, and I didn't try that again.  I let them win that round, that's for sure.

This was at the end of winter, about 25 years ago, I'd say.  I saw them one morning on my way to work.  They were lingering on the edge of a corn field.  There were about a half dozen loitering around a drain pipe, about ten of 'em in a half-dead oak tree 10-12 feet off the road, three of them on the tin roof of a pig sty staring down at the oinker and her piglets, and two more at the edge of the road, picking at a possum that didn't quite make it all

the way across.  Twenty-one or twenty-two of those so and so's.
And that was just the first day.  When I got down to the end of the
state road, I turned right onto the highway and passed the village.
The birds were there late that afternoon when I came home.  I
don't know if they stayed there all day or if they left and came
back.  Either way, they were there.

It had been cloudy that day, but it hadn't rained.  Weather
man said we had a 30% chance of rain.  I said it wasn't so.  We
had a 50% chance of rain.  Every day.  It was either going to rain
or it wasn't.  50/50.

Like I said, it didn't rain that day, but it did the next.
Wasn't raining when I left for work, but it sprinkled that evening.
As I drove down the road, those black birds were there in that
field.  I didn't count them, but it looked like a couple more had
joined the flock.  Some were on the tree, some were in the field.  I
saw several hopping around.  They were there again that evening.

The third day was rainy, too.  Heavy rains in the morning
and a drizzle in the afternoon.  There were no birds on the ground.
They were all in the tree.  About the same amount, maybe 1-2
more.  Most of them were on the bottom limbs, with fewer the
higher up the tree went.  Looked like a pyramid of black.  That was
the afternoon that I stopped the truck and got out.  I wanted to see
them up close, see what they would do.  They watched me from
the time I got out of the pick-up, watched me the whole way.  It
was unsettling, that's for sure.  I got about fifteen feet from them,
and that was as close as I wanted to get.  They didn't move.  I
didn't move either.  We just looked at each other.  Like I said, I
think they were testing me.  Testing me for what, I don't know.  I
talked to them.  "Hello, birds."  Nothing.  "What y'all doing here,"
I asked.  Nothing.  I stomped my foot.  Nothing.  I cawed loudly
like a crow.  Nothing.  If anybody had seen me, they probably
would've thought I'd flipped my gourd.  I had an air horn with me

that I kept in the truck for emergencies. I held it in my right hand and pointed it at the birds. Nothing. I pressed the trigger, and a loud blast came from the air horn. It hurt my ears. The birds all opened their wings and screeched at me, but they didn't fly away. I took my finger off the trigger. The birds stopped screeching and lowered their wings. They just stared at me again. Then one hopped down from the tree. Then another. Then another. They were glaring at me. That was when I ran back to my truck, turned the key, and sped back home. I didn't even look back.

I had nervous dreams that night, of black wings flapping in my face. I woke up, sweating, with the sheet over my head. I untangled myself and went to the bathroom. I urinated, washed my hands, then splashed cold water on my face. I looked in the mirror and saw my eyes were puffy. I laid back down and eventually drifted back off with no more dreams.

When I left for work that morning, which was the fourth day, the sun was just coming up, and there was a light mist. I decided to go the opposite way up the state road so I didn't have to pass the field. It took me about fifteen minutes out of the way, but I didn't care just then. On my way home, I was listening to Juice Newton singing "Angel of the Morning," and my muscle memory kicked in, I guess. I didn't think about where I was going and drove my normal way home. When I got closer to the field, I felt panicky, but I was almost home. I almost sped up, but the curves are tricky. I slowed down instead since there was no one behind me. As I approached the field, the birds were there, about 30 this time. One was chasing the big pig around the sty. Several others were picking at a rabbit, and the rest were either in or at the base of the tree. They all stopped what they were doing and turned to stare at me. The rain came down harder then, and I hit the gas, driving up the hill back to the house.

I checked the mail quickly, pulled down the driveway, and

parked in the garage.  I went into the house through the garage door, locking it behind me.  I kicked off my shoes and looked out the front window.  Just a couple of cardinals and a woodpecker.  I closed the blinds, went into the kitchen, and grabbed a beer from the fridge.

The fifth day was Friday, and I almost called in sick.  I hadn't missed a day all year, so I got my ass up out of bed and got dressed.  I wasn't gonna let some fowls scare me from my job.  The weatherman said the weekend was going to be beautiful, and the morning was already sunny.  I drove my normal way to work, and I was surprised to see no birds in the field that day.  I breathed a sigh of relief and continued on my way, hoping I'd seen the last of them.  I was wrong.

When I passed the village that afternoon and turned up the state road, there were more birds than ever.  The field looked black, there were that many.  Must have been a couple of hundred of those great black birds.  They were all standing on the ground facing me.  I pulled over to the side of the road and got out of the truck.  I had my camera in the truck, and I had to take a few pictures so that I could assure myself I wasn't crazy.  As I snapped the pictures, the birds started hopping up into the tree, one by one.  Pretty soon the trees were full of their black mass weighing down the tree.  I would swear I could hear the branches straining underneath all that feathery weight.  The birds all stared at me, then as one, they looked up into the sky, which had become gray.  I hadn't noticed when the sunshine left, but this was just plain spooky.  Several of the birds at the top of the tree, about a dozen or so, took flight towards the river.

I stood and watched, a little scared and a little excited.  I wanted to see what would happen next.  I took a step closer, and all the birds held their wings out in warning.  It was like a synchronized dance.  I stepped back, and the wings came down.  I stepped forward again, and the wings shot back up.  I took two steps back this time, finished with the dance.  The birds did not drop their wings this time, but instead lifted their beaks to the sky again and began crying.  It wasn't a caw like a crow.  No, this sounded like a baby crying out in pain.  It was loud, and it freaked me the hell out.  As the birds cried, the dozen or so birds that had flown away returned.  One by one, the birds flew over the tree and opened their mouths, dropping water to the earth.  When they were done, it began to rain, lightly, and in one huge mass, the birds flew away towards the south.  Their wings darkened the sky for a moment, and then they were gone.  I don't know what kind of bird they were, if they were even really a bird and not some kind of demon, and I never saw them again.

I went home, unnerved, and tried to heat up a can of soup, but I wasn't feeling hungry.  I turned on the news, and the forecast was still for sun, but it was raining outside.  A moment of realization kicked in, and I hopped in my truck and rode down to the village.  I parked in front of The Periodic Coffee House and looked out at the river.  The level of the river had significantly increased.  I ran inside the coffeehouse and called out to old man Keller, who came hustling out of the kitchen.  I told him about the river, but not the birds, and he walked outside with me.  We both looked up at the darkening sky and knew more rain was coming, despite the forecast.  He sent me down the street as he went inside to shoo out his customers and close up shop.  I went down to Miss American Pies and to Sizemore Meats before Keller caught up to me.  We were having a hard time convincing people, and we were losing valuable time as we had to keep coaxing them outside.  We finally got through the businesses when we flagged down Officer Thomas.  He immediately made the call to the precinct through his radio, and pretty soon the warning sirens were going off in the village.  People began moving items from the first floor of their houses and shops up to the second or third stories.  It took a lot of teamwork, and we didn't finish everything that day.  We worked well into the night, but we were all getting tired.  Neighbors helped neighbors, and friends and family were called in from outside the village.

By eleven pm, the rains were heavy, and all the streams were flooding as they became backed up trying to empty into the Ohio.  The river level had risen to 32 feet.  Flood level was 34.  I finally went home about 3 am to try to sleep for a couple of hours.

By 7 am, the river level was right at 34 feet, and water was beginning to drift over the retaining wall onto River Street.  We were back at it, getting people out of the village and taking what belongings they needed.  We were able to get a couple of the school busses from the village and load them up with people and pets.  There was an animal shelter on one of the side roads of the village, and we had moved them all up to the second level.  There were about 8 dogs and a dozen cats.  They were all in kennels and had food and water.  Stacy Henderson ran the shelter, and she refused to leave the animals behind, so she stayed with them.  We had too much to do to argue with her.

By noon, it was like a monsoon.  The wind was blowing at around 60 mph, and the rain felt like gravel as it hit you.  The river was over 36 feet now, meaning there was about 2 feet of water on the street.  We had waders on by now, but it made it all slower going.  Some of the water would wash down into the sewer, but the sewers became backed up.  Pretty soon there were sanitation issues as toilet wastes started flowing down the street.  Water was flowing into basements and into the first floors of homes and businesses, but at least all the residents were safe.  All except for Gilda Myers.  Her house had been dark, and no one answered the door Friday evening when we were making rounds.  We didn't know she'd had a stroke in bed Thursday night and was laying there dead.  We found her three days later.  Her bedroom had been on the first floor, and her body had taken on a lot of water.  It's not something I want to talk about, but that'll haunt me for a long time.

It rained all day Sunday, but not as hard as it had the previous day.  The river was at 39 feet now, 5 feet above flood level.  Half the village was underwater.  No one was allowed in.  Police, fire, and EMT did patrols in boats.  By Sunday afternoon, the rain stopped, and we all took a deep breath, but around midnight, another storm came through.  I was in my home, just up from the village and at a much higher level.

Denton County was in a State of Emergency, but there wasn't much that could be done until the waters receded.  I had to go to work Monday, and it was gloomy, but there was no rain.  Tuesday was sunny.  Some of the water began to evaporate, and some of the flood waters began to flow on down the Ohio.  By Thursday, the water was all gone, at least from the streets, but there was a nasty brown mud that covered all the roads.  Most of the basements in town were flooded and needed to be pumped out.  I helped where I could Thursday and Friday evenings, then all day during the weekend.  Some treasures were lost, and furniture and carpet had to be replaced.  A lot of drywall had to be replaced as well.  These things would take some time.  Insurance money would start to come in, and people would be okay, eventually.

As we were cleaning up trash from the streets and parks, I found a Polaroid picture on the merry-go-round in Nevile Park.  It was curled up, and most of the picture had been torn away.  What was left was just the face of a man with long brown hair and a beard.  He was wearing what looked to be a green t-shirt, and he was holding a cat, but it was hard to tell. It was the eyes that got to me, though.  It looked like he was staring right at you, you know, but it was just a picture.  Those eyes were sad.  I didn't know who it was, so I showed the picture to old man Keller.  I figured if anyone knew it was him, since all the locals came in to get coffee.

Ike didn't know, however, so I just tossed the picture away with the rest of the trash.  As damaged as it was, the picture wasn't really worth saving.

Nevileville was cleaned up, and life got back on.  Most of the people came back to live, but some had decided that the flood was the final straw.  It wasn't the first flood, and it wouldn't be the last.  Some people were tired of rebuilding and would move on.  Those that came back were helped.  We moved some of their stuff back down to floor level, and the businesses reopened.  I still think of those damned birds, though, and that loud cry.  I guess that cry was kind of like the village siren, a warning.  It got me moving anyway, and I'm glad of it.  We saved a bunch of people that weekend and saved a lot of their personal property, too.  Like I said, though, I haven't seen those birds in the last 25 years.  Not in that field anyway, but I do see them in my dreams.  Scary bastards, but I'm thankful for them.  I hope I never see them again.

# The Savior in the Coffee House

Lucy was watching the man alone sitting at the little round table, sipping his skinny caramel macchiato.  He was young, early 30s probably, with long brown hair and a trimmed beard.  He was above-average height, maybe 5'10" or so, and lean.  He wore a green faded Teenage Mutant Ninja Turtles t-shirt and khaki cargo shorts.  The sandals he wore were worn, and his feet looked dusty.  He looked familiar.  She tried to strike up a conversation with him when he first sat down.  "Oh, you like the Ninja Turtles, too?  My favorite is Donatello.  How about you?"

The man looked at her, and his eyes softened.  "Michelangelo, of course," he said with a slight smile.

"Of course," she had agreed.  "Who wouldn't love Michelangelo.  Cowabunbga!" she exclaimed.  The man smiled politely.  *"Cowabunbga?"* she thought, *"Really?  Geez, Lucy, get a grip."*  She took his order and asked if he wanted a cookie or pastry to go with his coffee.  The man politely declined.

He was now reading a discarded daily newspaper and looked troubled.  The front-page headline was "Hamas Takes Credit for Barcelona Bombing."  The man turned the page.  "Body of Missing Child Found Near Walnut Creek."  Page 3- "State to Add Referendum for Legalizing Marijuana."  The paper crinkled as he turned the page.  "Rosey and Trump are at It Again."  Ads.  He quickly turned the page.  "Televangelist to build $14.5 million mansion in Putnam County."  The man closed the paper, folded it neatly, and laid it on the table.  He wiped his eyes, playing it off like he had yawned, but Lucy had seen a tear.  The man then reached up to his ears and pulled out his earbuds.  Lucy hadn't noticed these before.  She had been thinking about her mother, who was having surgery in the morning to remove a tumor.

The man looked up at Lucy and smiled.  She was attractive, in a gothic sense.  She had brunette hair, which had once been dyed blonde but was now pink.  She wore heavy blue eye shadow, which did not detract from her bloodshot eyes.  She needed sleep, not caffeine.  Her black t-shirt read "The Periodic Coffee House" above a pocket that held her pack of Winstons.  The back of the shirt read "We drink coffee Periodically," in white font.  Her cut-off blue jean shorts were almost indecently short, but she covered her legs in black tights.  Her arms were tattooed with images of roses, dragons, and pentagrams.  She had a nose ring and several piercings in each ear.

Lucy walked from behind the counter over to the table and asked the man if she could get him anything else.

"Just the check, thank you," he answered.

"Here you go," she said, tearing the sheet from her pad. "That'll be $5.25.  By the way, if you don't mind my asking, what were you listening to?  I'm always looking for new tunes."

"Oh, you might say it was talk radio," he replied.

"Oh, yeah, I just like music," she said.  "Old school stuff, usually:  Bad Brains, Dead Kennedys, Helmet, Rage Against the Machine, you know.  That kind of stuff."

The man smiled again, warmly.  "Yes, I do know.  The music I listen to, though, is usually a bit calmer."

"That's cool," she said.  "I like the aggressive music

sometimes to help me stop thinking about my problems."

"I understand.  Henry Rollins is an interesting young man with a lot of deep thoughts," he said.  The man reached into his shorts pocket, pulled out a $10 bill, and handed it to Lucy.  "Keep the change," he said.

"Thank you very much," she said.

"You're welcome.  Have a blessed day," he said, standing up.

"You know," she started, "You look very familiar.  Has anyone ever told you that you looked like Jesus, that guy from The Walking Dead?  That's my favorite tv show."

The man's smile faded.  "Yes," he replied.  "Tom Payne.  I get that a lot.  My friends used to call me Jesus, too."

"Well, you should be flattered," she said.  "I mean, that man is hot!"  Lucy realized what she had said, and then her cheeks flushed red.  She was too embarrassed to say anything else.

"Well, I guess, thank you for that," the man said, smiling once again.  "Maybe you'll see me Sunday."  The man walked to the door.  As he opened it, the door struck a bell that chimed.  He paused and turned back around.  "And don't worry about your mother.  Everything is going to be alright."  Before Lucy could reply, the man had exited and began walking down the street.  A lightbulb went off in her head.  "My friends used to call me Jesus." That's what he had said.

Lucy dashed to the door, opened it, and raced down the street toward the man.  "Hey, wait!" she called.  The man hadn't gone far, just a few storefronts down, looking at a display window for the used book store, A Portal in Pages.  Stephen King, Clive Barker, Anne Rice, and Dean Koontz books stared back at him with images of blood, vampires, and rabid dogs.  He turned to her as she called to him, and the morning light shone fully on his face, nearly blinding her.

"Are you alright?" he asked.

"Yes.  I just realized that you *are* him.  Could I please have your autograph and get a selfie? She said, holding out her pen and order pad.  The man took the pen and pad hesitantly.  "Could you please sign it 'To Lucy,' and would you add 'My friends used to call my Jesus?'"

The man looked at her sadly but did as she requested, scribbling out some lines on the pad.  Lucy moved in close to him and held up her cell phone.  The man smiled slightly, but his eyes were sad.  Lucy pressed the button, and the image appeared on her phone.  He handed over the pen and pad to Lucy.  "Go in peace," he said softly.

Lucy beamed.  "Thank you, thank you, thank you!" she squealed.

The man turned, glancing at the book store display once again, before continuing down the street.  The cool October air blew a flyer for an exotic dance show past him, but he didn't look down.  He walked past a wooden power pole that had a crisis hotline number for opioid addiction.  Below that was another flyer, this one for a missing black cat.  Lucy watched as he turned the corner at the intersection, then she returned to the coffeehouse.

When she got back into the shop, she finally looked at the pad the man had signed for her.  As requested, the man had written "To Lucy.  My friends used to call me Jesus."  Below those words where she expected to see Tom Payne's signature was a symbol of a fish, an ichthus, followed by the numbers 3:16.  She would have to ask one of her friends what that meant.  It was probably a reference from the show, maybe season 3, episode 16.  She was a little disappointed, but it was still cool.  She would buy a small frame for it later that day and stand it on her nightstand by her bed, next to the picture she was going to have printed from her phone. Can you imagine her friends' reaction when she showed them the picture of her with Tom Payne?  They would be so jelly.

# Cilly

I don't know where she came from, and I don't know where she went.  She came in on a breeze and left on a whisper.  Just like that.  She was gone, and it was cold.

Her name was Celia, which I later found out was Latin for Heaven.  It was a fitting name.  She insisted I call her "Cilly," which was also fitting.  She was silly.  She was so wonderfully, wonderfully, wonderfully different.

Where she walked, the grass grew a little greener, and the weeds were replaced by flowers.  I know this cannot possibly be true, but, back then, it sure seemed like it.  She loved flowers, Edie Brickell, The Princess Bride, and, of all things, Jake "the Snake" Roberts.  It didn't make sense, but then it made perfect sense because, well, she was Cilly.  And that explained it all.

The only time I ever saw her without a smile was when she looked into my eyes.  She would look inside me.  I don't know what she saw, but she would blink and then laugh, like she had just heard the funniest joke.  She was infectious.

She would walk down the road and pick wildflowers.  When a car would approach, she would hold them out and yell, "Flowers for Peace!"  No one ever stopped to take the flowers she offered, but she didn't mind.  She shrugged it off, kept walking, and waited for the next car to come down the street.  She was hope.

When I first saw her, she was sitting in front of a wall-sized periodic table inside a coffee house.  She smiled and asked me what my favorite element was.  I didn't know if it was a strange pick-up line, if she was truly interested, or if she was just being Cilly.  I was caught off guard, of course, but I think that's what she wanted.  She always kept you on your toes.

"Tungsten?" I said, questioningly answering, my voice cracking a bit.

"Interesting," she said.  "Why tungsten?"

"I like wolves," I said.  "The chemical symbol for tungsten is W and is called wolfram in German.  It's a rare metal."  I felt like such a nerd, which I was, and I was sure my face was red, not gray like tungsten.

She stood and stretched.  She was long and pale and perfect.  "It is a pleasure to meet you, Wolfram," she said, extending her hand.

I shook her hand gently.  It was warm and smooth, and I wanted to hold her hand forever, but I let go before it became awkward.  More awkward.  She picked up her cup of coffee and began to walk away.

"Wait," I said.  "What's your name?"

"Cilly," she said, but I didn't know she meant her name.  I thought she was calling me silly.  "And I like tungsten, too."

I stood there, mesmerized.  I didn't know if I should run after her or just fall to the floor.  Play it cool, I said to myself.  Which is exactly what I did.  I ran after her.  I turned the corner, and she was gone, like a ghost.  I went outside and there she was, sitting in the grass on the village green beneath a maple tree, smiling.

"It's about time," she said.

I know I must have looked frantic and puzzled, like Einstein riding a bike.  She just looked at me and laughed.

"You called me silly?" I inquired.

"Of course not," she replied.  "Well, you are, but that's good.  What I meant was, I'm Cilly.  Short for Celia."

"Oh," I whispered.  "So, um, you like wolves?"

She didn't reply.  She just patted the ground beside her, and I sat down in the grass that was greener where she touched.

We talked for what seemed like days, but was, in actuality, a couple of hours.  We talked, we laughed, and I was comfortably uncomfortable.  She was fascinating, intelligent, and utterly frustrating.  She talked, and I listened.  She asked me questions, and I answered, doing my best to be charming.  Any questions asked of her would either be unanswered or just so ridiculously answered that you didn't know if she didn't understand, if she was brilliant, if she was insane, or if she was just being elusive.  In the end, I think it was a combination of them all.  She didn't want to talk about anything serious.  She wanted to have fun and laugh.  She wanted to hear funny stories.  She was like a queen, and I was her jester.  My purpose was to entertain, and I tried to do that.

I looked at her, and she was beautiful.  To quote Princess Buttercup, she had eyes "like the sea after a storm."  We talked on and on about The Princess Bride, about Westley and Buttercup, Fezzik, who was played by the remarkable Andre the Giant (who would one day wrestle against Jake "the Snake" Roberts), and, of course, Miracle Max and Valerie ("I'm not a witch, I'm your wife").  We talked about Rodents of Unusual Size (no, I don't think they really exist), and we talked about wuv, twue wuv.  I fell in love with her right then.  Years later, I think it was just the idea of her.  But right then, it was her.

I leaned in towards her, wanting to kiss her so badly.  She put a firm hand on my chest, and with a playful smile in her eyes, asked, "Whatcha doing?"

"I'm sorry," I stammered.  I was hoping to kiss you."

"Oh, a kiss," she said.  She pushed me gently back.  "As you wish."

She leaned into me, and I could feel her breath.  I closed my eyes.  She gave me a peck on my nose.  I jerked my eyes open, and she laughed.  "You are the devil of perturbations," she exclaimed.  She jumped up and ran around the tree, around me, over and over again, singing, "I'm not aware of too many things.  I know what I know, if you know what I mean, d-do ya?"  I got up, flabbergasted, and chased her, both of us laughing like crazy kids, which we were.

After a few minutes of the chase, I stopped, breathless, and leaned against the tree.  She snuck around and looked at me, seriously.  "What?" I asked.  She covered my eyes with her pale hand, leaned in, parted my lips with hers, and we had our first, and only, kiss.  It was like taking that first sip of coffee or hot chocolate; it warmed my stomach, my soul.  Whenever I drink a hot beverage these days, I think of that kiss, even after all these years  Again, I was breathless.  She drew back a bit, shyly.  I took her hand and leaned in, wanting another kiss.  She pulled back from me again.  "It wouldn't be the same," she whispered.  I thought she had tears in her eyes.  Then, all of a sudden, a smile returned to her face, and she was Cilly again.  "Who's your favorite wrestler," she asked.

We sat under the tree for another hour, and I made several futile attempts at kissing her again.  Each time she would say, "maybe later."  I didn't know there would be no later. After that hour, she proclaimed, "I'm starving. Are you hungry?"

"Yes," I replied, realizing that I was, indeed, hungry. "Do you want to go get something to eat?"

"No, I'll stay here," she replied. "Go get us something?"

"Sure," I said. "What do you like?"

"Surprise me," she answered with a twinkle.

I went back inside the coffee house and bought a couple of bagels and cream cheese. When I came back out, she was gone. There was a note on the ground where she had sat. Nervously, I opened the note.

"I'm sorry. I remembered I had to get home. I would like to see you again. Same time tomorrow? C," the note read.

I thought about Cilly all night. She haunted my dreams, my Buttercup. I kept looking at the clock to see if it was time to go back to the tree. It wasn't. I closed my eyes. Saw her face. Heard her voice. Felt her lips. Couldn't sleep.

At two o'clock the next afternoon, I rushed to the tree. Cilly was there, like she had never moved. She stood up and gave me a hug. She was soft and warm and smelled like Spring.

"I'm so glad you're here," she said.

"As you wish," I said.

She smiled. We talked. We walked. She picked flowers and tried to give them away. No one stopped. Cilly didn't mind.

I asked her where she lived. "Down there," she said, pointing down the road.

"Can I see your house?" I asked her.

She shook her head. "Not right now," she said. Momma's sleeping. She works nights. I asked her where her mother worked. Cilly gave me a flower. I tucked it behind my ear. Cilly smiled and held my hand.

We went back to our tree. We didn't say anything for a while. We just sat there and leaned against the tree and against each other. I looked at Cilly and her eyes were closed. She was smiling. She must have felt my gaze and she opened her eyes, dreamily.

"I love you," I said to her.

There was sadness in her eyes, for just a moment, and then she smiled again. "I'm thirsty," she said. "Would you please get me a Coke?"

"Of course," I said, standing up. "Will you be here when I get back?"

Cilly just looked at me with her smile and shrugged.

I went into the coffee house to buy a Coke. I looked out the window, and Cilly was sitting there. I ordered the drink, paid the barista, and walked back outside. Cilly wasn't there, but she had left another note:

"I'm sorry again. My mother called and said she needed me. Tomorrow? P.S. I love you, too. C."

I folded the note, put it in my pocket, and took a sip of the Coke. I was puzzled, of course, but she loved me. Cilly loved me!

It rained the next day. I didn't think Cilly would be at the tree, but I took my umbrella and walked there anyway. She wasn't there.  I waited half an hour, in the rain, but she didn't show.  I remembered a bit of verse she had recited to me.  "Raindrops and teardrops, just like the sea, falling from you down upon me."  I think she wrote it.  I don't know.  Cilly was and is a mystery.  I walked in the direction where she said she lived, hoping I might see her or she might look out the window and see me.  I didn't.  She didn't.  I walked home, sloshing through puddles.

It rained the next day, too.  I went to the tree.  Cilly wasn't there, but there was a note in a baggie, thumbtacked to the tree.  "Tomorrow?  C," it read.

The following day was sunny.  The ground was still wet, so I took a blanket with me.  When I got to the tree, Cilly wasn't there.  I went into the coffee house.  Cilly wasn't there, either.  I looked at the periodic table on the wall.  There was tungsten, element number 74, right between tantalum (Ta) and rhenium (Re), above seaborgium (Sg) and below molybdenum (Mo).  The letter W, wolfram, German for Tungsten, was circled in red marker.  All around the circle were drawings of red hearts and red flowers.  Next to the W was a plus sign, followed by a C.  Cilly.

I walked back outside and sat under the tree.  I wanted to cry but found I could only smile.  Cilly.  Strange, wonderful, beautiful Cilly.  I knew then I'd never see her again, and I never did.  She never came back to the tree.  There were no more notes.  There were no more doodles on the periodic table. I left her notes on the tree, but they were always there when I returned.  I looked for her, looked for her house.  I didn't know her last name, and it dawned on me that she had never asked me what my name was.  She would call me Wolfy, or Wolf-boy.  We talked, we kissed, we fell in love, and then she was gone.  In like a breeze and out like a whisper.

I didn't understand at the time why there was a periodic

table hanging on the wall, but the barista I questioned said that the owner used to be a chemistry teacher.  That was years ago, and the coffee house now doubles as a bar at night.  They have a small area in the corner where they will periodically (no pun intended) have spoken word or live music.  I have read my poetry there, and on a couple of occasions, I have played my acoustic guitar and sang a few tunes.  I've played "What I Am" and "Circle" by Edie Brickell, always thinking I'd look out at the audience and see Cilly sitting beneath the periodic table, but she's never there.  What is still there is that maple tree outside on the green, and I walk past it periodically (pun intended this time).  I don't sit beneath it anymore.  The grass looks a little greener underneath that tree.  At least is does to me.

# R.I.P. Andy Sizemore:  A Life in Signs

Our life is dictated by street signs.  I bet you didn't know it, but they are.  Unless you're a hermit, then maybe not so much.  But if you leave the house, if you go to work, if you go to school, if you go to the mall, if you go anywhere, then your life is dictated by street signs.  There are signs that tell you what road you're on.  If you're on a highway or interstate, signs tell you the mile marker, sometimes as a whole number, sometimes as 1/10 of a mile, and sometimes as 2/10 of a mile, which is really 1/5, but I digress.  There are signs that tell you what lane to be in, signs that tell you when to merge or yield, signs telling you that there is construction ahead, signs that tell you that road work ends, signs that tell you not to make a U-turn, signs that tell you to stop, signs with squiggly lines that tell you the road is curvy, and so forth.

I'll bet you don't know how many signs are on your commute.  I do.  Approximately 620.  I say approximately because signs are always changing and because, well, it's difficult to count signs when you're driving.  They make laws that tell you not to text and drive, yet they put up signs that they *want* you to read while you're driving.  Kinda ironic, right?  I'm not OCD.  I don't count signs because I have to.  I was just curious.  Once.

One morning on my way to work, after I passed the signs for The Periodic Coffee House, Jenny's Hair Salon, Miss American Pies, A Portal Through Pages, U-Store It, Lucky's Bar, and Killian's Pharmacy. As I got on the highway, I saw a new sign on the side of the road.  It was a cross, just off the shoulder of the road.  There was no one behind me, so I slowed down.  On the cross were the words, "RIP Andy 2017."  Below the cross were several single flowers; carnations and a couple of roses.  There was also a brown teddy bear with a white bow tie around its neck.  I made the sign of the cross and continued on to work.

I passed the sign for the exit ramp and past the "One Way" sign on the off ramp.  I passed gas station signs, other fast-food signs, and signs that indicated the speed limit and "No Parking Any Time."  When I got to work, there was a sign for my business, signs for short-term parking, signs for handicapped parking, and signs that read "Private Property No Trespassing."  I parked in a space without a sign and went into my building.

I didn't know who Andy was, but it nagged at me all day.  Between the emails and the phone calls, and the meetings, I thought about Andy.  I assumed he was a boy, and that he was a child, due mostly to the teddy bear.  As I drove home that evening, I barely noticed the 642 signs on my way home (Yes, there are more on the way home than there are on the way to work, for some reason).  After I popped a Hungry Man (Salisbury steak, corn, and mashed potatoes) into the oven, I sat down at the kitchen counter and opened my laptop.  After logging in, I pulled up my internet browser and searched "Andy 2017 death highway 52."  A second or two later, the search engine spit out 5,387 matches.  All I needed was the first one.  It was a news article from The Nevileville Daily.  I clicked on the hyperlink, and it took me to the newspaper article.  The article was short and read:

**Highway crash kills child, injures mother**

(June 24, 2017)

An afternoon crash yesterday on northbound Highway 52 near Fleming Drive took the life of 4-year-old Andrew "Andy" Sizemore.  The driver, Lucy Sizemore, sustained numerous minor injuries but was released from the hospital.  According to authorities, Sizemore was driving to the Funland Park when a baby deer ran out in front of the vehicle.  The driver slammed on breaks to avoid the animal, but wet road conditions caused the vehicle to slide off the side of the road and into a tree.  The child, who had been buckled, had removed the seat belt to pick up a toy he had dropped.  On impact, the child flew forward, striking his head on the windshield and causing his death.  No charges were filed against Mrs. Sizemore.



Andy Sizemore.  4-year-old child.  Taken way too soon, and for what?  A toy car?  A Lego block?  A Teenage Mutant Ninja Turtle?  Or maybe a teddy bear?  It was so sad, and I almost wished I hadn't searched the internet for his name.

I picked at my Hungry Man dinner, although I didn't feel too hungry.  I turned the television on to Wheel of Fortune and then Jeopardy, but I didn't really watch.  All the letters that Vanna turned over, and all the answers that Alex stated were Andy Sizemore.  I even dreamed about him that night.  He was a bright-eyed child with brown curly hair and an infectious smile on his face.  He called me by name.  "Hello, Mr. Franklin.  How do you do?"  Before I could answer, he ran off down the road, past the Speed Limit 35 sign, a brown faun with white spots following behind him.

Over the next few days, I noticed the sign each day on my way to work.  Every day I would make the sign of the cross and say a little prayer, for Andy, and for his family.  Eventually, I stopped noticing the cross.  It was just another sign along the highway, just like the "No U-turn," "Plant Entrance," and "Welcome to Lawton County" signs.

Summer turned into fall, and the leaves on the trees changed colors before falling to the earth.  On a rainy Saturday in October, I was driving up the highway, on my way to Snydersville to have breakfast at Waffle House.   I usually have coffee and a muffin at Periodic, but I had worked hard all week and decided to treat myself to steak and scrambled eggs with hash browns scattered and covered.  I don't know if it was the rain that caused me to remember, but for whatever reason, I thought about Andy.  I slowed the car as I neared his cross on the side of the road.  The teddy bear with the white bow tie was gone, as were the flowers.  You could still make out the RIP Andy 2017, but it was faded.  I couldn't make a U-turn because the sign told me not to, so I continued up to Fleming Drive.  I turned around there and crossed back over Highway 52 towards home.  Two miles from my home was a sign for Family Dollar.  I got in the left-hand lane, where there was a sign that read "Left Turn Only," and I made a left turn only.  I pulled into Family Dollar, shut off the engine, and went inside.  I purchased a black Sharpie marker, a plastic cemetery vase that stuck in the ground, a bouquet of plastic red roses, and a brown teddy bear.  The teddy didn't have a white bow tie, but it did wear a navy-blue vest.  I paid for the purchase, got into my car, and drove back up Highway 52.

At Mile Marker 16.4, I stopped the car, put on my hazard lights, and retrieved the plastic bag from the store.  I also took some restaurant napkins from my glove box.  It had stopped raining.  Kneeling before Andy's cross, I carefully wiped the rain and grime from the cross.  After I removed the Sharpie from the package, I carefully retraced the words and filled them in so that it was once again legible.  I drove the vase into the dirt next to the cross and placed the plastic roses in the vase.  Finally, I placed the teddy bear beside Andy's cross, fastening it with a piece of string I had in the car.  Once everything was in place, I crossed myself and said another prayer for Andy and his family.  Cars passed by behind me, but I barely heard the noise or felt the rush of wind as they sped by.  I spoke to him then.

"Hello, Andy," I whispered, "I saw you didn't have your teddy bear anymore, and I thought you might want a new one.  God bless you, little one."

I don't know why, but a tear came to my eye, and I let it fall.  I stood up and wiped the dirt and gravel from my knees.  I got back into my car and drove on towards Waffle House.  On the way there, I passed Zion Baptist Church.  A neon sign there read, "God is in control."  I figured He was.  I figured He had sent the rain to remind me about Andy.  I'm glad He did.  Not all signs are street signs.

# **<u>Lucy</u>**

## <u>1</u>

Lucy Sizemore wasn't a religious woman. It wasn't all her fault, and it didn't make her a bad woman. She did volunteer work. She was a good person. She tried to make her little corner of the world a better place. For her community. For herself. For Andy.

She had tried going to church for a while. She didn't not believe in God. She was just unsure of things. There were too many bad things in the world. Too many killers, rapists, child molesters. She had heard about the scandals in the Catholic church. Priests drinking and having sex parties. Groups of priests making kids undress and posing like Christ on the cross while they laughed and took pictures. Priests that had their way with children, boys and girls. How could you trust the church when this was the moral compass? If God was nowhere else, surely He was in the church, and if this was going on in the church, well…

Lucy was not a religious woman, but she did see God, every time she looked at Andy. He was such a beautiful child, almost an angel. He was always so happy, always smiling. She had thought she'd known true love before, but she had been wrong. Andy was true love.

Lucy had grown up in Nevileville. Her dad owned the butcher shop, and her mother was a seamstress. They weren't rich by any means, but they always had food and clothes, even if neither was ever the freshest. When she got into high school, she

started hanging with the goths and stoners.  She liked the clothes.
She liked the music.  She was listening to Black Flag, the Dead
Kennedys, Rage Against the Machine, Helmet, Bad Brains.  All
the classics.  She wore mostly black, wore a lot of eye makeup and
lipstick, and pierced just about everything she could pierce.  Her
hair color changed about every couple of weeks:  sometimes jet
black, sometimes red, sometimes purple.

She was a good kid.  Her parents didn't understand her look
or her taste in music, but she didn't give them a hard time, and she
made decent grades.  Lucy was never going to be a doctor or a
rocket scientist, but she was going to be okay.

When she turned 16, Lucy got a job at the Periodic Coffee
House in the village.  Mr. Keller was intrigued by her, not because
he was a pervert who liked young girls, but because she was
unique.  Lucy was a warm, caring person, and she was outgoing.
She could talk to anyone and made friends easily.  Even the older
people who came into the coffeehouse loved Lucy.  She had a way
of making people look past the exterior.

In the fall of her 18th year, a man came into the
coffeehouse.  It was early in the morning, and the place was empty.
He sat down and ordered a skinny caramel macchiato.  He looked
familiar to Lucy, and she realized after a while that he was an actor
on the tv show, The Walking Dead, her favorite show.  She had
gotten an autograph from him and taken a picture with him on her
camera phone.  She had made a couple of 4"x6" copies of the
picture.  One was framed and sat on her nightstand, and the other
was framed and sat by the register.  She talked about that for weeks
until her friends got tired of hearing about it.  They *were* jelly, just
as she thought they'd be.

She had worked for Mr. Keller for 3 years when Job
walked in.  He was not from the village.  He was a student at UC

and was studying sociology and creative writing.  He was a poet and had come down to Nevileville for the Spoken Word Night the coffeehouse held every two weeks.  He had dark hair that was shaved on the sides and hung down in the front.  He had tattoos up each arm, studs in his ears, and a tongue piercing.  The piercing wasn't the only thing that was silver.  Job had a way with words.  He was a poet and a charmer.  When it was his turn at the mic, he spoke with passion and authority.  When his voice grew soft in a whisper, everyone strained to hear.  When he looked at Lucy, he smiled.  She smiled back and blushed.

Job waited for her that night as she cleaned and closed the coffeehouse.  He wanted to talk to her more, but there wasn't much talking.  They couldn't go back to her parents' house, so they drove down the highway and parked behind a restaurant that had been closed for years.  He took her virginity that night, in the back of his Focus.  She hadn't told him he was her first, not then.  It wasn't how Lucy had imagined her first time, and it hurt, but it was good, and he was sweet.

Job didn't have a cell phone.  He didn't like the thought of signals beaming down into his head or people hacking into his calls and texts.  With Lucy busy at the coffeehouse and Job busy with school, they saw each other mostly on Spoken Word Nights.  They spent more time in the back of the Focus than they did talking to each other, but that was okay.  Lucy loved him.

Two months after they had first met, Lucy realized she was late.  She took a test, and it came out positive.  She was scared, but she knew she had to tell Job.  A week later, after the Spoken Word, they made love behind the abandoned restaurant again.  When they were finished, Lucy got up the nerve to tell him.  Lucy didn't know how she expected him to react, but his eyes and mouth widened.

"Are you sure?" he asked.

"Yes," she had told him. "I took a second test, just to be sure." She started to cry, and Job took her in his arms.

"Shhh," he said, lovingly. "It's okay. We'll take care of it," he assured her.

"What do you mean, 'we'll take care of it?'" Lucy asked.

"We can go to the clinic," he said. "You know, Planned Parenthood. We'll take care of it. It'll be okay."

"You want me to have an abortion?" Lucy asked.

"Well, yeah. Isn't that what you want? I'm in school, and you work at a coffeehouse," Job replied.

"I don't know," Lucy said, quietly.

"What do you mean you don't know?" Job said, his voice rising. "We can't take care of a baby."

"I don't know," Lucy repeated.

Job made plans to take Lucy to the clinic a week later. When they got there, Lucy wouldn't get out of the car.

"I can't do this," she said.

"What? You have to!" Job exclaimed.

"Job, I can't. I love you, and I want to have the baby."

"Are you kidding me? I thought we were on the same page! I came all the way down here for this? What do you think we're going to do?"

Lucy cried. "I'm sorry Job. I can't do it. Please don't be mad. I love you."

Job softened, and he sighed. "It's okay," he said. "I love you, too."

The next week, Job wasn't at the Spoken Word. Lucy had no way of getting in touch with him at the college, and she was scared. Job came down to the coffeehouse three days later, on Friday morning. The morning coffee rush had cleared out, and it was a little too early for lunch. Lucy beamed when he walked in.

"Job!" she squealed. "I was afraid you weren't coming back. Where have you been?"

Job hugged her and gave her a kiss on the forehead. "I'm sorry I wasn't here Tuesday," he said. "I was busy at school and couldn't get down here until now."

"It's okay," she said. "I was just worried, you know? I thought you were going to leave me."

"Lucy," Job started. He looked at her, and there was hesitation in his eyes. The he smiled. "I've got some great news to tell you."

"Yeah?" she said, expectantly.

"Well, the reason I wasn't here Tuesday was because my creative writing professor called me to his office. I had applied for a study abroad program, and I got accepted! Isn't that great!"

"Study abroad? What do you mean?" Lucy asked.

"I will get to spend the next six months in England and France, studying literature there. It's a full grant. Flight, room and board, meals. And they'll pay me $300 a week for incidentals! I get to go to Europe for free, and they're going to pay me!"

Lucy turned away and started to cry.

"What?" Job asked. "Aren't you happy for me?

Lucy turned back to him, her eyes watery and red. "You're leaving? What about the baby?"

"Lucy, it's only for 6 months. I'll be back before the baby's born. I promise. Then we'll get married. I've worked it out with the administrator at UC. You can stay in the dorm with me!"

"I can't believe you're leaving," she said quietly. "I thought you loved me."

"Lucy, I do love you, but this is the chance of a lifetime. And I'll be back. I promise," Job said again.

"When do you leave?" she asked through her tears.

"Monday," he said.

"That soon?" Lucy asked.

"Yes, I've got to go right away. I've got so much to do. I have to pack and everything. They are doing a rush on my passport. It's crazy!"

"Yes, it is," Lucy replied.

"I've got to go, Lucy. I love you. I'll call you when I get there so you can have my address and phone number."

"Wait, I'm not going to see you before you go?"

"You're seeing me now. I've got a lot of packing to do. I told you."

"Oh," Lucy said, hollowly. She turned and walked toward the kitchen.

"Lucy?" Job called.  Lucy didn't turn around.  She just walked into the kitchen and let the door close behind her.

<u>2</u>

Job didn't call.  Lucy never saw him or heard from him again.  She called once to the UC administrator's office and was placed on hold.  When the receptionist came back on the line, she said, "I'm sorry, but we have no record of a student named Job Barnes, and we have no partnership with a study abroad program."

Lucy cried all day.  When her parents questioned her, Lucy finally told them about Job and the baby.  Her dad was angry, but more at Job than he was at Lucy.  Her mother held her, and Lucy cried on her shoulder.  They were going to take care of her and the baby.

They tried several times to find Job, but he had become a ghost. Lucy had never seen a driver's license, so she didn't even know if Job was his real name.  God, she had been so stupid.  He had told her everything she wanted to hear, and she had fallen for it.  She had fallen for him.

The Kellers were very generous with Lucy.  When she sat them down at Periodic, she expected them to fire her.  Who wants a pregnant waitress, right?  Especially an unwed pregnant waitress whose boyfriend had run out on her.  It was too scandalous.  Lucy was wrong.  The Kellers were much more understanding and supportive than Lucy imagined.  They told her that she would have a job there as long as she wanted, and if anyone gave her a hard time, they would have to answer to them.  They even gave her an extra dollar per hour raise on top of the tips she received.  The

Keller name was respected in Nevileville.  Sam's father had been a chemist before he retired and then a chemistry teacher at the high school, until he retired again to open the coffeehouse.  After he and his wife passed away, Sam took over the coffeehouse.  This had been a few years ago, before Lucy had turned 16.  The Kellers were good people.  They were like family.

The weeks went by, and the baby grew inside Lucy.  Her parents took her to every doctor's appointment.  The baby was healthy.  The sonogram showed that it was a boy.  Lucy wasn't sure if she wanted to know the sex, but she thought it best so she could start preparing.  She and her mother began shopping for clothes at thrift and consignment shops.  Her mother taught her to sew so that she could mend anything that was ripped along seams.  The Kellers had a baby shower for Lucy at the Periodic, and many of the regular customers attended and brought gifts.  It was a surprise shower, and Lucy was truly surprised.  She had no idea about the shower, and she certainly didn't expect so many people to turn out to a party for her.  She was moved by the love shown by her friends, family, and community.  They all supported her.  Who needed Job?

The baby was breach, and the doctor had to perform a C-section.  He came out crying, but that was okay.  He was healthy, and this time, Lucy truly was in love. She named him Andrew, the real name of the actor that played Rick Grimes on The Walking Dead.  Andrew Lincoln.  He was the leader of the group on the show.  For his middle name, she chose Thomas, which was the name of the Jesus character from the show.  It was also the man she had met that day in the coffeehouse.  Andrew Thomas Sizemore.  A noble name.  A strong name.  8 pounds, 3 ounces.  A beautiful, healthy baby boy.  Andy.

Andy's crib was in Lucy's room in her parents' house.  She had taken down all the puck rock posters she'd had on the walls and replaced them with posters of Disney characters and Noah's ark. It was a good story. The Kellers gave her as much time off as she needed before she went back to work at the Periodic. Lucy's mother worked out of the house, so she was available and willing to keep little Alex.

Lucy was making decent money at the coffeehouse between her hourly pay and the generous tips, but she wanted more for her and for Andy. She began taking online classes through the community college. She thought she could do medical billing and documentation and work for a doctor's office. She had talked with the women at her gynecologist's office, and they loved working there. The pay was pretty good, as were the benefits.

When she wasn't working at the coffeehouse, Lucy was either working on her online classes or spending time with Alex. As he grew, she would take him to the park to play on the slides and swings or to the waterpark in the neighboring town. While she did okay and scraped by in high school, Lucy had a renewed purpose, studying hard and making A's in her college courses. She graduated with honors with an Associate Degree. Ironically, there was an opening at her gynecologist's office; one of the ladies there had left to work at the Children's Hospital. She had a short interview with Dr. Susan Leeds, who hired Lucy on the spot. She would start working in two weeks. Her official start date would be June 26.

June 23 was Lucy's last official day working at The Periodic Coffee House. That evening, the Kellers had a going-away party for her. She had been a mainstay at the coffeehouse for 6 years, and she would certainly be missed. Sam Keller told Lucy that there would always be a spot there for her if she ever needed to return or if she wanted to work on the weekends. Lucy thanked Sam, and there were hugs and tears all around. And there was cake.

Lucy woke up early on Saturday, June 24. She was a new woman with a new life! She had a new job that she would be starting in two days. She was going to be able to afford to move out of her parents' house soon, and Andy would have his own bedroom, and so would she. Not that she wanted a man, but she did want her own space. It was hard a lot of times having a toddler as a roommate. She had to be quiet when he was sleeping, and she would either have to make him leave the room or go to the bathroom to change clothes.

She woke Andy up and made him breakfast: bacon and toast with butter and strawberry jelly. They had a busy weekend planned. Today they were going to the amusement park just up the highway. They would ride some rides, play some games, eat ice cream and cotton candy, and stay until nightfall to watch the fireworks. Tomorrow they were going to Johns Lake State Park to have a picnic and go swimming.

They left the house at 8:30. The park opened at 9, and Lucy wanted to get there early to get a good place to park to beat the crowd. It had rained during the night, and the sky was still cloudy, but there was no rain in the forecast. Andy and Lucy were both buckled. Safety first! She turned on the radio. Instead of her punk CDs, Lucy turned on an FM station that was playing 80's music. Crowded House was on. She sang along as Andy sat in his car seat in the back seat. He was playing with a toy he had brought along for the ride. Michelangelo, the Teenage Mutant Ninja Turtle.

"There's a battle ahead. Many battles are lost, but you'll never see the end of the road while you're traveling with me," Lucy sang. "Hey now, hey now, don't dream it's over."

Andy cried in the back seat, "Mommy, I dwopped turtwle."

"Where is it?" Lucy asked.

"On the seat," Andy replied.

"Okay," Lucy replied.  You can unbuckle real quick and pick it up.  Hurry up and get buckled back."

"Okay, Mommy," Andy said.  He pushed the button and pushed the arm up.  He couldn't quite reach Michelangelo, so he crawled over onto the seat.

Lucy was watching Andy in the rear-view mirror.  Coming up on Fleming Drive, a baby deer ran out into the highway.  It was young and still had its spots.  Lucy slammed on the brakes and swerved.  The road was wet from the rain, and the car skidded.  She swiped the deer and the car went hood first into a tree on the side of the road.  Andy flew forward, and Lucy's head hit the steering wheel.  Her world went black.

Lucy woke up to bright lights and a throbbing head.  She heard crying and saw her mother and father sitting by the bed.  They were hugging each other.

"Mom?" Lucy asked.

Her parents got up and came over to the bed.  Her mother took her hand.

"Where am I?" she asked.  Then she remembered Andy.  "Where's Andy?"

<u>**3**</u>

Lucy had been released after tests had been run and shown that she had no serious injuries.  She was urged to talk to a therapist.  Lucy was in a daze.  Andy.  It was her fault.  She never should have let him get out of his seat, but it was only for a minute. It was her fault. All her fault. Oh God. Oh, Andy. I'm sorry. I'm so sorry.

She didn't go to work that Monday. Dr. Leeds understood. Let her take as much time as she needs, she told Lucy's mother. Let us know when she's ready.

The viewing was on Tuesday evening, and the funeral was on Wednesday. Because of the village laws, Lucy's parents had arranged for Andy to be buried up in Grover, two towns over. Everybody was supportive and offered condolences, but Lucy felt like everyone was looking at her and whispering behind her back. "It was her fault." "She did it". "She killed her little boy". "How could she do something like that?" "Not surprising, she was just a whore anyway. No husband, no boyfriend." "Look at her hair. Does she even know what color it's supposed to be?" "I bet she sets off every metal detector with all those piercings". She could hear them all. Every word. She saw the looks. They were all judging her. They all hate her. She knew none of that was really true. The people of the village had always supported her and her family. She just hated it all right then. She hated herself.

Lucy locked herself in her room. She didn't come out for a couple of days, except to go to the bathroom. Her mother and father tried to talk to her, but Lucy wouldn't talk. She turned off her cellphone so she wouldn't get calls or texts. All she wanted to do was cry and sleep. Andy.

Her parents made one last attempt to find Job Barnes. They wanted him to know that he had had a son, and he was now gone. They Googled his name but didn't find any good leads.

A week later, Lucy came out of her room. She was hungry. She had a dorm refrigerator in her room where she kept a few bottles of water and snacks, but it was empty now.  Her face was swollen from crying.  Her mother made her pancakes.  Lucy ate a few bites, but that was all she could eat.

Lucy's father suggested they make a little memorial for Andy on the side of the highway where he had died.  Lucy thought it was a good idea but didn't know if she could do it.  Her dad had gone to the hardware store and picked up some wood and had made it into a cross.  Lucy cried again and hugged her father.

Later that day, Lucy asked her parents to go for a drive and place the memorial.  On the way, they stopped at the grocery store, where Lucy bought a small brown teddy bear that had a white bow around its neck.  Her mother bought a few carnations, white and yellow, and a couple of red roses.

When they arrived at the spot near Fleming Drive, Lucy wouldn't get out of the car.  Her father and mother left her there and walked over by the tree.  The tree was intact, but there was noticeable damage where Lucy's car had hit.  Lucy's father pushed the point at the bottom of the cross into the damp soil and adjusted it so that it was level.  Across the frame of the cross it read: "RIP Andy 2017."  He stood up, wiping the tears from his eyes.  Lucy's mother placed the flowers in front of the cross, fanning them out.

Lucy's father came around the side of the car and opened her door.  He was holding the teddy bear in his hand.  "It's your turn," he said softly."  Lucy sighed and got out of the car.  She walked slowly to the little memorial.  She knelt in front of the cross, reading the words.

"I'm so sorry, Andy.  I love you.  I wish it was me and not you.  I'm so sorry."  She placed the teddy bear in front of the cross on top of the flowers.  Lucy got up quickly and ran back to the car, crying.

## <u>4</u>

A month passed.  Lucy never went to work at the doctor's office.  They eventually hired someone else.  The Kellers checked in on her to see if there was anything they could do.  Lucy wouldn't see them.  She couldn't.  She wouldn't leave the house.  There was no one other than her parents that she could face, and she could barely face them.  She covered her mirrors so she wouldn't have to face herself.

Lucy lost weight because she hardly ate.  She wasn't heavy to begin with, but now she was beginning to look sickly.  She was pale, and there were large bags under her eyes.  If she turned on the television, it was usually to the Cartoon Network, which had been Andy's favorite.  Lucy didn't care about The Walking Dead anymore, either.  She was just a walker now.

On August 12, Lucy woke up from a dream.  She had seen Job.  He was sorry.  He had gone to England and France, but he was back.  He knew about Andy, and he was sorry, so sorry.  He was there for her now.  He would always be there for her from now on.  Could she forgive him.

Yes, Lucy thought, I can forgive you.  She knew where he was.  She quickly dressed and quietly went downstairs.  She took her father's keys and went out the front door.  Fortunately, the door did not squeak.  She got in the car and started it up.  Before pulling away, she looked in the glove compartment.  It was there, her father's Glock.  She knew he always kept it in the car, just in case.  Well, just in case was now.

As she turned on Highway 52 and went south, the radio

played.  It was George Thorogood.  He was bad to the bone.  Damned straight, Lucy thought.  I know just where you are, you lying, deadbeat son of a bitch.

She pulled behind the abandoned restaurant where they had fooled around so many times in the back of his Focus.  His car wasn't there.  Job was nowhere to be seen.  Lucy waited.  Job wasn't coming.  He never was and never would.

Lucy held the Glock in her hands.  She thought about Job and Andy, and she cried, loud, violent cries.  She couldn't do this anymore.  She didn't want to do this anymore.  She placed the barrel of the gun in her mouth and pulled the trigger.

<u>5</u>

She opened her eyes.  Lucy Sizemore wasn't a religious person, but she was a good person.  She was happy and outgoing and everyone loved her.

There was a man standing in front of her.  She knew him.  He had long brown hair and a beard.  He wore a faded Teenage Mutant Ninja Turtles t-shirt and khaki cargo shorts.  He had kind eyes, and he smiled at her.

"Tom?" Lucy asked.

The man continued to smile at her as he held out his hand.  "My friends used to call me Jesus."

Lucy took his hand, and he helped her out of the car.  Her fingers entwined in his, and they started to walk down the highway.

"Where are we going?" Lucy asked.

"Home," Tom replied.  "We're going to see Andy."

Lucy smiled and whispered, "Andy."  She squeezed Tom's hand tighter, and they continued walking.

# <u>Mr. Liar</u>

## <u>1</u>

Some nicknames are really good nicknames, and they add a coolness factor or a mystique to the individual.  Most times you know the person just by their nickname.  In baseball, you have name nicknames like "The Georgia Peach," "The Sultan of Swat," "Moonlight," and "The Iron Horse."  In football, there's "Crazy Legs" and "The New York Sack Exchange."  In hockey, there's "The Great One" and "The Kid."  In movies and music, you have "The Gipper," "The King," "The Queen of Soul," and "The Velvet Fog."  What did they call me?  "Mr. Liar."

My friends thought it was funny.  They knew I didn't like it, and the more I showed my dislike, the more they used it.  Mr. Liar.  I run in a circle of artistic people.  Sireen is a folk singer and plays guitar.  Lucian and Jenny are painters.  Tina is a ballet dancer.  Pete is a photographer.  Mackenzie is a poet, and Vic is a biographer and history writer.  Me?  I write novels and short stories.  Fiction.

It was Vic that gave me the nickname.  We were all meeting up at Lucky's one night, and I was the last to arrive.  As I strolled in, Vic turned and announced, "There he is, Mr. Liar!"  Everyone at the table turned and looked at me, laughing.

"What are you talking about?" I asked.

"Mr. Liar.  That's you, bro!"

"What did I lie to you about?

"Oh, you didn't lie to me, man. You lie to everyone about everything. You're a writer."

"Whoa," I said, offended. "That's not cool. Mac and Vic are writers, too."

Pete piped up now. "Yeah, Jay, but they tell the truth. You just make up shit," he said with a grin.

I pointed at Mac, "Nuh uh," I said like a 3-year-old. Mac makes up shit, too."

Lucian spoke up with his freaky-deaky half French, half German accent. "Not true. Mac's like a painter. She writes what she sees. She describes the world."

"That's what I do, too," I said, finally taking off my coat.

Tina leaned over to me and gave me a hug. "No, love. You *do* make shit up, but it's beautiful shit."

I had to smile in spite of all this. Tina had that way. She was classically cute, a graceful dancer, and she gave great hugs. I knew my friends weren't being malicious. They thought Mr. Liar was apt, and I guess it was kind of cool. And it did ring with a bit of truth. I was a fiction writer. My stories were inspired, but they were, for the most part, made up. I had written two novels that had been published, and I was working on a collection of short stories. Mr. Liar. I guess there were worse nicknames.

Mackenzie's nickname was Mac. Not a great nickname, just a shortened version of her name. She was a bit on the heavy side, but nobody dared to call her "Big Mac." There were certain things you just didn't do. That and the fact that her partner was bigger than her, and she would chokeslam you through a table. Really. Mac's partner, Billie, was a professional wrestler who went by the ring moniker "Veronica Valhalla" and dressed like a

Viking.

Sireen's name was cool all by itself, so we usually just called her by her name.  Because she was a singer with a hauntingly beautiful voice, we referred to her as Sireen the Siren.  She loved playing and singing Janis Joplin, Alannah Myles, and Sheryl Crow.  She was better than all of them, and her shows were always packed.

Lucian's nickname was "Frenchy."  He hated it, but we liked pissing him off.  He wasn't French.  He was originally from somewhere near Austria.  He had studied art in Paris, and he was fluent in 4 languages, but he could be understood in none.  Especially when he was mad.  That's why calling him Frenchy was so funny.  He would get ticked and start spouting off in sentences that mixed English, French, German, and Spanish.  Sometimes he would throw in a word in Portuguese.  You never really knew what he was saying, but you knew he was cussing you.  When he wasn't cussing you, Lucian was warm and caring.  He would always ask how you were feeling, and he was truly interested.

Jenny's nickname was "Tutone."  Not surprisingly, her nickname came from the song, 867-5309 (Jenny) by Tommy Tutone, which came out in 1981 before any of us were born.  Jenny had heard the song on an oldies station and had fallen in love with it.  She would sing it all the time and would request the song whenever we were in a bar listening to live music.  Some musicians acquiesced her request, if they knew they song.  When it would play, she would dance and sing the chorus as loudly as she could.  Jenny is a hoot, a free spirit.

Tina's nickname was "Tink."  The nickname was close to Tina, and she loved Tinkerbell.  She was a big fan of the Disney character and had Tinkerbell shirts and posters.  She even wore her hair cropped like Tinkerbell.  She was my secret love, and she was the person I centered many of my female characters around.

Pete was a nature photographer.  His photos had been published in National Geographic, Birds and Blooms, and in many other books and magazines.  Though he was primarily freelance, he did a lot of work for the Cincinnati Zoo.  We called him Click. I had originally called him "Snapper," but everyone hated that nickname.

Vic was "The Professor."  He did not yet have his doctorate, but he was working on his dissertation.  He had written presidential biographies about Ulysses S. Grant, James A. Garfield, and Woodrow Wilson.  He had also written a book about abolitionism in Denton County and the particular part that Nevileville played.  He wore scholarly glasses and looked like a professor.

How we all became friends really doesn't matter, but artists tend to flock to each other.  We were creative.  We were creators. We were the gods of the page and the stage, the palette and the portrait.  I think we all found each other because we had a way of building each other up.  Sure, we could tease each other, and we did, but in the end, we critiqued, and we critiqued with love.  If something didn't look right, sound right, or read right, we told each other, constructively.  We were honest with each other, even me, the liar.  We would tell each other what other friends, family, or lovers would not.  We made each other better, and we supported each other.  If Sireen played a show, we were there.  If Tina danced, we were there.  Photo galleries, art shows, poetry and book readings.  Yep, we were there.  We even went to Billie's wrestling matches.

## <u>2</u>

I made out with Tina once.  We had all been drinking, and I walked her home.  She couldn't unlock her door, so I took the key and let her in.  She took my hand and led me inside.  I closed the door, and she kissed me.  I had wanted this for so long, and I kissed her back.  She backtracked to her bedroom, kissing me the whole way there.  She unzipped her dress and let it drop to the floor.  Standing there in her bra and panties, she was beautiful in the sliver of streetlight that peeked in through the window.  Even as drunk as she was, every move she made was graceful.  She stretched out on the bed beside me, and we kissed some more.  I moved my lips down to her neck.  As I gently kissed and licked her neck, I felt her hand go slack on my back and heard a low snore.  Tina had passed out.

I got up out of bed, moving to her side, and gently lifted her legs to pull the covers down.  I covered her up and laid down beside her in case she became sick during the night.  As tired as I was, I had a hard time sleeping, as I kept thinking of Tina and her kisses.  I would watch her sleep and wonder what would happen in the morning when she woke.

Around 8:30, Tina stirred, which woke me as well.  She opened her eyes and was startled to see me there.  It took her a moment to realize it was me and not a burglar or killer.

"Jay?" she asked, blearily.  "What are you doing here?" She looked under the cover.  "What happened last night?  Did we…?"

"I stayed over because you were drunk and passed out," I said.  "I just wanted to make sure you were okay."

"And nothing happened?" she asked.

"Oh yeah," I grinned. "Three times."

"Oh, God, really?" she said with a groan.

Feelings hurt, I replied, "No, not really. You don't remember anything?"

"The last thing I remember is you walking me home and me trying to unlock the door."

"Oh, okay. Well, nothing happened after that, Tink. We were going to have coffee, and you came back to change," I lied. "When you didn't come back to the kitchen, I checked on you to make sure you were okay. You were lying on the bed, and I covered you. I only stayed because I didn't know if you would need me during the night. You know, if you got sick or something."

"My hero," Tink said, smiling. "Can you imagine if something had happened," she said, and I thought I heard disappointment in her voice, but that could have been my ego. "That would've been awkward."

"Yeah," I replied. "Awkward."

We looked at each other for a moment, then Tina got up out of bed. She wasn't shy about being in her underwear in front of me. I guess it was from all the quick changes dancers have to do backstage.

"I'm going to take a shower and get ready for rehearsal," she said. I have to be at the theater at 11. Do you want to stay and have that coffee after I'm done?"

"No, thanks," I said, although I wanted to stay more than

anything.  "I have to go home and write for a few hours."

Tink floated over to me and put her arms around my neck. "Thank you for taking care of me last night," she said, kissing me on the check.

There were so many things I wanted to say to her.  Instead, I just said, "You're welcome."

As I was leaving Tink's, I saw Mac and her partner, Billie, walking their Pug down the sidewalk toward me.  My first instinct was to dash off, but I knew I had been seen.  I raised my hand in a wave and waited for them to catch up.  Mac had a shit-eating grin on her face, but Billie just scowled at me.

"Taking the walk of shame, are we?" Mac teased.  "Shame, shame, everyone knows your name."

"No, it's not like that," I told them.  "Tink was drunk, and I walked her home last night.  Nothing happened."

"Nothing, huh?" Billie snorted.  "Then you must have been using Tina's lipstick."

"What?" I asked, wiping my lips.  Sure enough, there were traces of red lipstick on my fingers.  If Mac and Billie had seen it, Tink must have also.  "It was just a goodbye peck, that's all," I told them, as I turned and headed home.  I could hear them laughing as I walked away.  "Shame, shame, everyone knows your name." That was two years ago.

<u>**3**</u>

We began hearing rumors about some company buying up properties in the village.  We saw it firsthand in February, when Lucian moved to Paris.  He had been offered an artist-in-residency at a college there.  Before he could put his house on the market, a representative from an investment company called and offered him a very generous price.  Of course, Lucian accepted.  He was the first of us to leave.

Mac and Billie were next.  Mac took a teaching position at a college in the Dayton area, which was almost an hour and a half away, too far for a commute.  Billie was a warehouse forklift operator by day, and she already worked halfway between Nevileville and Dayton, so there were no issues there.  She could still chokeslam people at night.  They wanted to leave on their own terms, and their lease was up.  This was in April.

By this time, the used book store and the butcher shop had already closed down for good.  The village had lost a lot of tax revenue since the power plant closed a year and a half ago, and many people in town couldn't afford tax hikes.  Streets and parks were not being maintained; the village just didn't have the money for the upkeep.  There were few shops in the village and even fewer events to draw shoppers and tourists.

Pete left in May.  He was going to be gone for 9 months to do a shoot in Africa for National Geographic.  His lease was up on his apartment anyway, so he wasn't really affected, other than having to get a company to move his belongings out of storage, since U-Store-It was bought and sold in September.  When he came back to the States, this was all gone. Nevileville was all gone.

Sireen, Jenny, and Vic all moved on, too.  Sireen was invited to play on a summer folk festival tour, with artists like Jewel and K.D. Lang.  She ended up moving to Nashville.  Jenny opened an art gallery in Cincinnati.  She did lessons and would also do those wine and paint events where everyone got drunk and painted the same picture.  Nothing wrong with that, I guess. Artists have to eat. Vic received a grant to do research for a book on Gettysburg.  He moved to that area to do his work.  That just left Tink and I.

After our one "night" together, we hardly were alone together.  Most of our time was around the rest of our group.  It was awkward, and we didn't talk about it.  She was offered a role as Rumpleteazer in Cats for a touring company.  She toured the United States, Canada, and Europe, and was gone for 14 months.  She was made an offer on her house while she was in London, and she called me to see what was going on.  We had all been corresponding via a group email, so she knew that some of the others had already sold and gone.  She wanted to know what I was going to do.  I told her I was going to do what I did best and always did.  Lie.  She laughed at that, but it was strained.  She really wanted to know what I had planned.  I told her honestly that I was still looking at options.  I had finished my collection of short stories and had been offered a 3-book deal from my publisher.  It was good money, but not Stephen King or Brad Meltzer money.  I could write anywhere, but I thought I wanted someplace warm.  Someplace like Charleston, South Carolina.  She said that Charleston was a wonderful place with a lot of history.  She thought I would like it.

Tink took the offer the investment company made her, and so did I.  Everybody did.  There wasn't much left of the village anyway, and the money was very good.  To paraphrase Joni Mitchell and the Counting Crows, they were going to raze paradise and put up a golfing course. Ooh bop bop bop.  We weren't going in a big yellow taxi, though.  Just moving vans.

She came back in September, a month before the sale would happen.  I picked her up at the airport and we drove back to the village.  It had changed a lot in the 14 months she was gone. There were a lot of vacant houses and businesses, and there would be more.  She started to cry, and I held her hand.  When we got to her house, she said she wasn't ready to go inside, so we walked down to The Periodic Coffee House.  The coffeehouse and Lucky's Bar were about the only places left open, and they would be closed, too, in a month.

We went inside, and the familiar bell chimed when we entered.  Sam Keller greeted us and told us we could sit wherever we wanted.  There were only a few other people inside.  Sam's wife was in the kitchen, and there was an elderly man sitting with what I assumed to be his grandson.  The boy's hands were bandaged.  The old man noticed me staring, and he nodded at me. I nodded back, then looked away. At the counter, we ordered black coffee and a piece of pound cake each.  There were no more pies. Miss American Pies had closed in June.  We sat at the table, and Tink put her hands in mine.

"Everyone's gone," Tink said.  "They all moved away and left us."

"I know.  Times have changed.  At least they're all on Facebook and Twitter."

"Did you see that Mac and Billie are adopting?" Tink asked.

"I did.  I'm very happy for them."

"Me, too," she replied.  We were silent for a couple of

minutes.  *Me and Bobby McGee* came over the radio.  "Freedom's just another word for nothing left to lose."

"Sireen sings this so well," I said, listening to the words.

"She really does.  Right over there, do you remember," Tink said, pointing to the corner of the coffeehouse where acoustic acts and spoken word had been performed for a few years.

"I do remember.  She was too loud for this place, but she tore the place down."

Tink smiled, but then her face went dead serious.  "What are you going to do, Jay?  Are you still going to Charleston?"

"I am, November 1.  I already signed a lease on a 2-bedroom cottage near the beach.  I'll write my novel there.  What are you going to do?"

"Well," she said, sheepishly, "I hear Charleston has a pretty good ballet company.

She looked at me, and when I said nothing, she leaned in and kissed me, not a friendly kiss, but a real kiss.  I returned her kiss, which was perfect. "I've been waiting to do that again for two years," she purred.

"Wait, what do you mean again?" I asked, puzzled.

"I remember that night," she said.  "You were a gentleman, and I was scared.  I was afraid if we did anything else that it would ruin our friendship.  I've thought about it every day."

"I have, too," I agreed, "it took everything in my will to be a gentleman that night."

She kissed me again.  We didn't care that the old man and his grandson were watching.  We didn't care that Sam and his wife were watching.

"Come to Charleston with me," I blurted.

"I'm playing the Sugar Plum Fairy in the Charleston Ballet," she said, with tears in her eyes. "I signed with them last week."

We held each other as we cried.  Sam shooed us away and told us our coffee and cake were on the house.  We were giddy as teenagers as we walked back to Tink's house.

Inside, Tink whispered in my ear, "You don't have to be a gentleman now."

**<u>4</u>**

We had most everything packed up, and Tink left two weeks before I did.  She had to begin rehearsals for The Nutcracker, but our cottage wasn't ready yet.  She stayed with one of the other dancers before we could officially move in.  I stayed behind and took care of all the last-minute packing and cleaning. The coffeehouse was closing on October 27, so I stopped in for a last cup.  Sam and his wife asked about Tink, and I told them she was doing well, and I would see her in a couple of day.  I showed them the small box with the diamond ring inside.  I was going to propose after we walked into our cottage.  They were happy for us. I was happy.  For the first time in a really long time, I was happy.

The moving van left on October 30.  It would take them 2 days to make the trip.  I was driving straight through, so I left on

Halloween.  It was fitting.  The morning was grey and threatened rain.  The village was a ghost town.  The fire and police departments and emergency services were patrolling the town, making sure that everyone had left or were in the process of leaving.  I nodded to them as they passed by my house while I was getting in the car.

I drove past Tink's old place and past Mac and Billie's house.  As I made my way through the village to the highway, I saw a man standing on the sidewalk looking out at the river.  He had long brown hair and a beard.  Despite the chill, he wore sandals, khaki shorts, and a faded green Teenage Mutant Ninja Turtles t-shirt.  He looked either homeless or lost.  He waved to me, and I slowed the car.

"Good morning," he said.  His voice was deep, and there was authority in that voice.  "Is it time to go?"

"Yes, sir," I replied.  "Do you need a ride somewhere?"

"No thank you, son," he answered, even though he looked to be just a couple of years older than me.  "My ride will be here soon."

"Okay, then," I said.  "Have a good day."

"You, too," he replied.  "Be safe and take your time.  She'll wait for you."

I nodded at him and rolled up the window.  Crazy old homeless man, I thought, as I turned onto the highway.  It took me a little bit longer, but I did drive carefully.  The man was right, though.  Tink was waiting for me, and she said yes.  Even though I would continue to write fiction, I promised myself I would never lie to Tink, and I didn't.  I left Mr. Liar back in the village, where they razed paradise and put up a golfing course.  Ooh bop bop bop.

# <u>Vital Vinyl</u>

## <u>1</u>

Louann Spicoli stood on the sidewalk by her shopping cart flinging albums into the Ohio River. The sky was overcast, there was a drizzle, and it was fitting, since she was singing Led Zeppelin's Fool in the Rain to herself, and to the geese and ducks who happened to be below on the river bank. "And the clock on the wall's moving slower. Oh, my heart it sinks to the ground. And the storm that I thought would blow over clouds the light of the love that I found, found," she sang, carefully taking the long player out of the sleeve. "In Through The Out Door," she thought. Underrated album. She held the black vinyl record in her hand lovingly, took a last look at it, then threw it, frisbee-style, towards the river. The album caught a breeze and floated, like all good Zep records should, sailing far and landing on top of the water about a hundred yards out. She watched wistfully as it floated away.

She picked up the next album. Kiss' 1979 disco-rock album "Dynasty." She loved this album, remembering when it first came out. Everyone thought it was a departure from classic Kiss and a sellout, but not Louann. While "I Was Made For Loving You," was the big hit, she was partial to "Sure Know Something." As the took the album out of the sleeve, she looked at the pictures of the Star Child, the Demon, the Space Man, and the Cat. Her tears were masked by the rain as she sang, "I was seventeen, you were just a dream. I was mesmerized, I felt scared inside. You broke my heart and I still can feel the pain." She took turns kissing the lips of Paul, Gene, Ace, and Peter, dropped the sleeve into the cart, and flung the album.  It didn't go as far as the Zep record, physically and metaphorically, but it still landed in the river, and she watched it float away, too.

Playing deejay, Louann announced, "Next up is the smash hit from The Oak Ridge Boys' 1981 album, 'Fancy Free.'  This is 'Elvira.'"  She took the record in her hands and did a dance where she bounced/squatted a couple of times as she sang, "Giddy up oom poppa omm poppa mow mow," before chunking the record.  It slipped out of her hand and rolled down the bank, scattering the geese, who let out noisy honks.  "Heigh-ho Silver, and away," she called, laughing hysterically as the record came to rest next to a piece of drift wood.  "I wonder if that's oak," she thought, laughing again at the potential irony.

## **2**

Louann always loved music.  She grew up listening to Led Zeppelin, The Beatles, Kiss, and Pink Floyd.  When Joan Jett came out with "I Love Rock 'n' Roll," in 1982, she didn't realize it was a cover of The Arrow's song.  She learned that later when she started selling records, but it didn't matter in 1982.  She was 13, and knew she wanted to be a guitarist.  She convinced her parents to buy her a used Stratocaster for her birthday, and she started wailing away, scaring the neighborhood dogs and cats into hiding.  She was terrible, but she was trying, and she was learning.  She did chores and earned money to buy music books to learn theory and chords.  When her parents saw that she was really into playing, they signed her up for private lessons.

Her teacher was a 19-year-old, long-haired kid who worked

in the music shop in Elmwood, just up the river from the village. His name was Owen Finkle, but his friends called him "Fink." He could play "Eruption" like nobody's business, and he had his own band that played Van Halen, Aerosmith, and Quiet Riot covers.

Louann was good at math, and she took to music easily. It wasn't long before she was flying through arpeggios and making Fink look like a fool, boy.

When she turned 15, Louann's parents bought her a brand new Les Paul guitar. She was still taking lessons from Fink, although he was starting to learn from her. For her birthday, Fink gave her some picks, a black leather guitar strap, and a set of Ernie Ball strings. He also took something from her, right there in the private lesson room with her mother sitting on the other side of the door. Fink had been taping lessons, and he played the previous week's tape so they wouldn't be heard. Louann's mother never knew. At the time, Louann was excited by the attention of an older boy. Man, actually. He had recently turned 21. Today when she thought about it, she shuddered. Perverted child molester, taking advantage of a young girl. "Eww," she thought.

<u>3</u>

She thought about Fink as she pulled an album out of the shopping cart. Winger. She cringed as she thought of the song, "Seventeen." She didn't even sing aloud as she thought of the lyrics, "Daddy says she's too young, but she's old enough for me." *Dirty bastard,* she thought. She didn't even take the record out of the sleeve. Instead she threw the album on the ground. As the weird, Picasso-esque triangle stared up at her with its laser beam and clock-like eyes, she stomped on the album, crunching it. She jumped up and down on it four times before she decided that was enough for Mr. Kip.

Reaching back into the shopping cart, Louann brought out Ike and Tina Turner's "Workin' Together." This was the album that featured their remake of CCR's "Proud Mary." Louann laughed out loud again and pretended to dance like Tina Turner. She didn't have Tina's legs, but what the hell? "Big wheel keep on turnin'. Proud Mary keep on burnin,'" she sang, pulling the LP from the jacket. "Roll on, Ike," she cried. "Roll on, Tina!" She frisbee-tossed the album as hard as she could. It sailed way past Zeppelin. "We have a winner!" she yelled, laughing.

## 4

Louann kept up with the guitar and her "lessons" and started a band that played school dances and talent shows. The band was horrible, but Louann was the star. She would take extra solos during their songs, which ticked off the other members of the band, as they thought she was hogging the stage, which she was. It was justified, she thought, since the rest of the band sucked, especially the singer, who was still going through puberty. Every time he would sing a high note, his voice would crack, and the crowd would crack up. The band didn't last long, though, as Louann couldn't take them anymore, and the rest of the band couldn't stand her showing them up.

One day after her 17th birthday, Louann went to the music store for her lesson with Fink. She arrived 10 minutes early, by herself. When she opened the door to the lesson room, she saw him with his pants around his ankles. He was with another girl from high school, a girl that wasn't even 15. "Louann?" he said, shocked. "You're early." Louann couldn't say anything, as the tears started rolling down her face. Her face hardened, and she gave him the middle finger as she picked up her guitar case and stormed out of the music shop. She went back home, slammed her bedroom door, and put the guitar case under her bed. She wouldn't play it again for over 30 years.

<u>5</u>

Wednesday evenings in the village were slow, but there were a few people milling about at the coffeehouse or at Lucky's, and Louann was drawing their attention. It wasn't every day that you saw a middle-aged woman singing to herself and flinging records into the river. Some of the folks stopped and had their phones held up, recording the rantings of a crazy lady. Surely, these would end up on YouTube, Facebook, and Twitter.

Louann was oblivious to this, but Sam Keller was not. He stood at the door of The Periodic Coffee House and watched with sad eyes. He knew Louann and had gone to high school with her. He knew she used to be a gifted guitarist, but he didn't know why she'd given it up until a couple of years ago. Louann came into the coffeehouse all the time and had struck up a friendship with Lucy, the waitress and barista there. Despite their difference in age, they were kindred spirits and had both been jilted by men they'd loved and trusted. Louann had told Lucy everything. Lucy, not trying to gossip, had innocently talked to Sam about her, not knowing that Sam did not know the history. When Louann found out, she was mad at Lucy at first, but she cooled down because she knew and trusted Sam. He was one of the few men she trusted.

Louann picked up a Willie Nelson album. Chunk. She

grabbed Madonna's "Like A Virgin." *Yeah, right,* Louann thought. Fling. The Cars, Public Enemy, Megadeth, Elvis. Fling, chunk, toss. Nobody knew it, but the Ohio River was getting a hell of a concert.

Sam opened the door to the coffeehouse and stepped outside. He moved to where the people were loitering and recording and ushered them away. There was no argument; when Sam Keller asked you politely to do something, you did it. He was that kind of person, as had his mom and dad been, God rest their souls. People respected Sam, and they moved away, quietly going about their business. The videos didn't surface on the internet or social media. This was river business, and the village took care of their own.

The crowd dispersed, Sam went back to his own business, leaving Louann alone. She never noticed. Poison, TLC, Marvin Gaye all sailed through the sunset.

<u>**6**</u>

Though she gave up the guitar, Louann Spicoli still loved music. She would listen to records, then cassettes, then CDs all the time. "Purple Rain" became one of her favorites. She loved 80s music: Culture Club, Duran Duran, Crowded House, Bon Jovi, Motley Crue. She had a diverse pallet. She went to college and majored in broadcasting, then took a job at a classic rock station as a weekend deejay. Eventually she landed a full-time gig and became a popular radio personality. On Thursday nights, she hosted a show from 9-11 called Metal Messiah, where she played everything from Cinderella to King Diamond, Alice Cooper to Slipknot. It was one of the most popular radio shows at WROX.

She didn't use her given name on the air.  Instead, she used the name Jani Lawless, a combination of Warrant singer Jani Lane and W.A.S.P. front man Blackie Lawless.  When she did radio promos at local businesses or went to concerts, people were always drawn to her like she was a celebrity, which she was, but on a minor scale, like the tv weather person.  She would take pictures with fans, sometimes sign autographs, and give out promo CDs, t-shirts, and concert tickets.

Louann partied with the rock stars when they came to town, either at the amphitheater or at the larger arena.  She hung out with Metallica, Rush, Iron Maiden, Guns 'N Roses, Def Leppard, all the big guns.  She drank, smoked, and snorted with them, among other things.  She wasn't a groupie, but that didn't mean she didn't act like one.  One night she passed out on the Crue's tour bus in Cincinnati and woke up in Kansas City.  No big deal.  I know it's only rock and roll, but I like it.  She called her boss and said she was sick, and they'd have to fill in for her that night.  No big deal, until it became a habit.

After a couple more similar incidents, the station manager called her into his office.  The Human Resources manager was there also.  Never a good sign.  Louann looked like shit.  She had bags under her eyes, her nose was red, and her shoes didn't match.  It was only rock and roll.  The station manager warned her to clean up her act, but Louann just laughed at him.

"I'm Jani Lawless," she told him.  "I have the highest rated show here, and you need me!"

The station manager looked at her and shook his head.  "You are Louann Spicoli.  Jani Lawless is a fantasy, and you're trying to live it.  No matter how much you party with the boys, you are not one of them.  You are an on-air talent, not an on-stage one."

Louann glared at him and literally snarled.  "Fuck you," she said.  "I quit."  She got up to leave, but as she did so, the world went spinning, and Jani Lawless died.

## <u>6</u>

She sang "Gonna be some sweet sounds coming down on the nightshift," as she hurled The Commodores album towards the water.  This was followed by Cindy Lauper's "She's So Unusual," and U2's "Rattle and Hum."

She sang and she laughed, but she was far from happy.  She was closing up shop.  For nearly twenty years, Louann had owned Vital Vinyl, and now it was over.  The man was sticking it to her, again.  It was always the man, right?  At least she was profiting from it this time.  If you're gonna get screwed, at least get paid.

## <u>7</u>

Louann woke up in Our Lady Hospital.  She had an IV in her hand filling her with a clear liquid.  She was dehydrated, and she had overdosed.  Cocaine and vodka.  She was lucky to be alive, she was told.  She wanted to be dead, she thought.

The station manager came to see her, and he was sympathetic.  He offered to let her keep her job if she cleaned up her act.  Louann thanked him and told him to fuck off.  He didn't fuck off, but he did leave her alone.

The police informed her that no charges would be filed

against her if she went into a rehab program.  She was pissed, of course, but she knew that no drugs was better than an orange jump suit.  It wasn't easy, but she did recover.  It took her awhile, and twenty years later she still struggled.  There were a couple of times in the beginning that she relapsed.  She had tough mentors that helped her through it.

Louann had managed to save a pretty good bit of money.  Most of the drugs and booze she imbibed weren't her own.  She wasn't a rock star, but she partied with them, and they always were carrying.  Because she was high most of the time or passed out, she didn't have to spend a lot on groceries.  Score!

Knowing she couldn't go back into radio, she decided to open a vintage record shop.  Vinyl was coming back into style, and she bought out a couple of vendors at a flea market south of Dayton.  She also built up her inventory by going to yard and estate sales and thrift stores.  There was a vacant building in the village that was perfect.  The rent was good, and it included the apartment above the store.  This would save her money as well.

Vital Vinyl was open for business in 1998.  Louann had a very good selection, and she was able to find for customers what she didn't have at the store.  She still had a lot of connections.  The grand opening went well, but Louann found that she couldn't make a living with just records.  She began selling t-shirts, posters, and comic books, and that helped out a lot.  Vital Vinyl became known as the place to go in the tri-state area for music.  She even had a radio advertisement on her old station.

## <u>8</u>

"Let me take you to town, and I'll show you everything that I know.  And I'll never let you down 'cause my love is like a merry go round," she sang, as Aerosmith's "Toys in the Attic" went flying.  She kept singing, "A woman's only human.  You should understand.  She's not just a play thing.  She's flesh and blood just like her man," as Aretha's "I Never Loved a Man the Way I Love You," caught air.  Louann was getting tired.  Flinging records was more of a workout than she'd expected, but she was almost done.  One left.


## <u>9</u>

In the winter of 2017, Louann's landlord, Virgil Wilkes, informed her that he would not be renewing the lease.  She had five months remaining on the current contract.  When she asked him why, Wilkes stated that he had received a sizable offer on the building, and he intended to take it.

"Shit!" was Louann's first thought.  Her second thought was, "What am I going to do now?"  Her third was, "I need a drink."  Louann hadn't had as much as a beer in nearly twenty years, yet she found herself in Lucky's Bar.  She ordered a Budweiser draft and took a sip.  It was bitter, but it was cold, and it was full of memories.  Not all of them good.

"You don't want to do that," said a voice.

Louann turned to see Sam Keller standing beside her.

"What if I do?" she asked.

"If I thought you really did, I'd leave you alone," he replied. "Why don't you put that down and come have a cup of coffee?"

"Hey, mind your business and stop stealing my customers, asshole," Lucky, the bar's owner, yelled from behind the bar."

"Keep the change," Sam said, tossing a twenty-dollar bill on the bar. Lucky grumbled but took the money. "You coming?" he asked Louann. He held out his hand, and she took it.

Sam probably saved her life that day. They sat and talked about her store, the lease, and the village itself. Sam had heard the rumors. Someone was buying up the village. Taxes and rents had increased. It was a matter of time before Nevileville would be a ghost town. This was four months ago.

Today was the end of April. Almost time to close up for good. Louann had tried to sell the business, but the offers were few, and for pennies. She called on some of her connections and found a job at a radio station in Dallas. She was leaving in three days. Today she was cleaning house, and it was bitter. She was blowing off steam, and it was okay. At least her tears weren't in her beer, and they never would be again.

## 10

Louann pulled the last album out of the shopping cart. The cover showed a band on stage in the background, with curtains on either side. The bottom half of the cover was green and had a gray path snaking from the side of the cover up to the stage. In white lettering it read, "One More For The Road," only the "For" was crossed out and "From" was inserted.  Lynyrd Skynyrd, recorded at The Fox theater in Atlanta in 1976 before the plane crash killed Ronnie Van Zant, Steve Gaines, and Cassie Gaines.  A double album.  14 songs.  She read the song titles on the back of the album.  "Tuesday's Gone with the wind," she said.  "Sweet Home Alabama.  Call Me The Breeze.  Gimme Three Steps.  Free Bird.  Crossroads.  Saturday Night Special".  Louann was at a crossroads.  This was it.  She whispered to the wind, "We crossed a bridge, and I took that gun and sailed it through the air.  I said, 'Ever been to Texas?'  She said, 'I think I'd love it there.'"

Louann looked down at the shopping cart.  There were no records left, just the empty sleeves.  Except for the album in her hands.  She clutched the record to her breast, smiled, and walked back into Vital Vinyl, leaving the shopping cart on the sidewalk by the remains of Winger.  She locked the door behind her and turned the sign to CLOSED.  The light in the apartment upstairs came on, and the bedroom window opened.  A minute later, there was the sound of an amplifier being turned on and up to 11.  A fury of notes flew out the window into the darkening sky, followed by the unmistakable opening notes of Free Bird.

On the bank of the river, the geese and ducks bristled at the cacophony and then settled down amongst the brush.  Robert, Jimmy, John, John Paul, Paul, Gene, Ace, Peter, Ike, Tina, and the rest of the apostles rolled on downed the river.  Outside The Periodic Coffee House, Sam Keller Stood, listening to Louann's guitar.  Though the amp was loud, he thought he could hear Louann singing along: "And if I stayed here with you girl, things just couldn't be the same.  'Cause I'm as free as a bird now, and this bird you cannot change.  Lord, help me, I can't change."

# **<u>Lucky</u>**

Nobody called him Paul anymore, not even his wife, Carmen.  Everybody knew him as "Lucky."  He was the owner of Lucky's Bar, and he was an asshole.

Paul Green had been a construction worker.  He had completed high school, taking classes at the vocational school.  He was a welder by trade and could lay a bead with the best of them.

While on a job site for a new office building up the highway in Ayers, the foreman had given him the keys to the forklift and told Paul to drive a load of concrete block over to the building frame they were erecting.  When Paul told him he had never driven a forklift before, the foreman said a few choice words to him, showed him the controls to lift and lower the forks, and told him to get moving.

Paul hopped up on the seat and inserted the key.  He pressed the brake, and the forklift started.  He raised and lowered the forks to practice, then drove over to the pallet of blocks.  He inserted the forks into the rungs of the pallet and pulled the lever down to raise the forks.  *No problem*, Paul thought.  The stack of blocks was tall, and Paul could not see over them.  He was going to have to raise them to the third floor anyway, so he went ahead and raised the pallet and started forward.  The ground had not been graded yet, so it was unlevel and bumpy.  As Paul neared the building frame, the forklift came upon a rut in the ground.  He turned the wheel to veer around the rut, and the swing of the forklift changed the stability of the load, causing the forklift to tip over.  The forklift came equipped with a seatbelt, but Paul was not wearing it.  The forklift also did not have an overhead guard.  When the forklift toppled, Paul was thrown from the vehicle.  The blocks, which had not been properly secured to the pallet, fell in all directions.  Several landed near Paul, and one landed directly on his head.  Fortunately for Paul, he was wearing a hard hat at the time, which saved his life.  The impact, however, did cause severe damage to his C1 and C2 vertebrae.  He would be in the hospital for two months and had another 4 months of physical therapy.

OSHA investigated the lost work day case and cited Vanguard Construction with numerous violations, including lack of training documentation, improper use of safety equipment, walking/working surfaces, unguarded floor openings, and fall protection violations.  The construction site was shut down for 4 days while the OSHA inspector investigated, looking at training records, maintenance and service reports, and equipment inspection logs.  In all, Vanguard was hit with $35,000 worth of fines, which their attorney negotiation down to $7,500.  The construction company had 30 days to comply with the action plan and address the violations.

A lawyer met with Paul in the hospital to go over their suit against Vanguard.  Paul had a good case against the company, especially after the OSHA citations.  Paul's lawyer petitioned for $3 million in damages for physical and mental anguish and for lost wages.  Vanguard settled for $600,000 and paid Paul's medical expenses.

His friends started calling him Lucky, not only because he had survived the incident and was on his way to making a full recovery, but also because of the substantial payout he had received from Vanguard.  While it wasn't enough for him to retire comfortably on, it allowed him to start up his bar in the village.  Lucky's Bar.

As the only watering hole in the village, Lucky's was instantly popular.  He had 20 beers on tap, a cooler full of domestic and premium bottled beers, and a large variety of liquor, top shelf and otherwise.  Lucky knew his clientele was the blue collared working man, so he kept his prices low and ran daily specials.  He had a dozen TVs stationed around the bar so that he and his patrons could watch any baseball, basketball, football, or hockey game.  He would order the pay per views and charge covers for people to watching boxing, UFC, and wrestling.  He would host NFL draft and fantasy football parties.  Business boomed.

Most of the bar goers were Bengals fans.  Every Sunday and on the occasional Monday or Thursday night, while everyone was wearing their black and orange, Lucky would sport the black and gold, the colors of the Pittsburgh Steelers.  He didn't care that the Steelers had won 6 Super Bowls, more than any other team, and 6 more than the Cincinnati Bengals.  Truth be told, he wasn't really much of a football fan, but he knew that wearing the colors of the Bengals rival would piss people off and more people would come to the bar to watch the games and try to shut him up.  Lucky was indeed an asshole, but it worked.  The bar was always packed for college football games on Saturdays and NFL games on Sundays.  The crowd would be decked out in Buckeyes, Bearcats, and Bengals shirts and jerseys.  Small groups of Patriots, Cowboys, and 49ers fans would also watch the games there, and they took a lot of heat.  Fortunately for those fans, their teams won more than the Bengals.  Most times it was hard to be a Bengals fan.  It had been a long time since Ken Anderson, Cris Collinsworth, Icky Woods, and Anthony Munoz.  A long time and a lot of losses, but not as many as the Browns, thank God!

Business was doing rather well.  Not booming, of course, because this was just a little village, but even in a little village, people had to drink, am I right?  During the football offseason,

Lucky did other things during the week to bring in business. Monday nights he would show WWE Raw. One of his customers, Billie Kingman, who went by the ring name "Veronica Valhalla," had made an appearance on Raw one time when the WWE was in Cincinnati. She was beaten by another big woman named Nia Jaxx, who gave her a big splash for the pin. It was a hell of a match seeing those two big broads go at it. Tuesdays was 2fer Tuesday. Two for one draft beers, whiskey shots, and appetizers from 6-9. There were always a bunch of hungover Nevileites come Wednesday morning. On Thursdays, Lucky would have team trivia nights, where the winning team would win a $200 bar tab. There were always at least 15-20 teams on trivia nights, so those were good nights. Lucky also brought in Keno from the Ohio Lottery. When things were slow, he would sometimes play. He once won $1,000. When he won, he used one of his catchphrases, which could mean good or bad, depending on the tone. "How do you like *that* shit?"

Lucky was vulgar. He wasn't a sailor, but he had a mouth like one. Sometimes if someone got offended, he would use the excuse, "Hey, I got hit on the fucking head in a construction accident. It gave me fucking Tourette's, alright, asshole? Is that okay with you?" A lot of the regulars loved Lucky's antics. If the Reds or Bengals lost, he would jump around like Casey Stengel dancing on hot coals with a swarm of bees in his dungarees. He would cuss up a storm and drop more bombs than a B-52. Most of the patrons tried to get him started. It was free entertainment.

Lucky's vulgarity even rolled over onto his menu. He served the Cincinnati-style chili, which on the menu was a "Bowl of Shit." If you had it with spaghetti noodles, it was a "Bowl of Shitty Limp Dicks." If you had a chili dog, it was a "Shit Dog." Sometimes on football Sundays when the joint was packed, Lucky would yell out, "Hey! Any of you assholes find a band-aid? I think I lost it when I was stirring the chili," then he would bust out laughing in a high-pitched cackle. Lucky's was not a family environment, but the food was damned good.

It didn't matter what the topic of conversation was; Lucky had an opinion. Politics? "They're all a bunch of thieving assholes. They'll both screw you. The Republicans will fuck you and make you pay them to do it. The Democrats will fuck you, tell you it's good for you, and have a bunch of immigrants line up to fuck you too." Sports? "The Bengals suck, but the Brown suck worse. They call themselves the Dog Pound, but that fucking place should be a kill shelter!" Religion? Yeah, I believe in Jesus. I saw the guy once. Walked right into the bar wearing khaki shorts and a Teenage Mutant Ninja Turtles t-shirt. Can you believe that? I asked him what he wanted to drink, and he said he didn't drink alcohol. He just wanted to know if he could use the phone. I told him that the phone was for paying customers only, asshole! He nodded at me and left, but I think the sissy was crying! Not much of a savior, if you ask me." Someone would always ask, "Who do you think Jesus was going to call?" "How the fuck do I know, I'm not an operator!" he would reply. "Maybe Ghostbusters or Master Splinter!"

The bar did well until 2017. The electric plant up the river closed down, costing the village a lot of jobs and tax money. Many of the villagers had to relocate to other parts of Ohio, Kentucky, and West Virginia if they wanted to stay with Avery Energy. Without the taxes from the electric company, the village sought to raise property taxes. This didn't sit well with the remainder of the villagers, and many of them started selling off as well. Of course, the loss of a lot of the blue-collar jobs hurt Lucky's business, as well as other businesses in town. Sizemore Meats, the local butcher, closed first. Some of it had to do with the property taxes, but some of it had to do with the loss of his grandson and daughter. Miss American Pies shut down, also. The rent had nearly doubled, and the business moved to Northern Kentucky. Then the offer came.

A man in a suit with a briefcase came in one morning just as Lucky was opening. He presented a business card and said he represented Azalea Holdings, LLC, and they were interested in buying not only his bar, but his house as well. Lucky, thinking this was a joke, told the man to go do something with himself that the man thought impossible, but he persisted. He assured Lucky that this was no joke and produced a contract. Lucky looked the document over, and his eyes widened. He told the man he would have to talk with Carmen about the offer. The man nodded and said he would call in a couple of days. Carmen didn't hesitate and told Lucky if he didn't take the offer, she'd divorce him. Lucky had to think about that one, but three days later, he signed the contract. The bar would be closed in three months.

Now Lucky was finished packing, and it was time to go. The moving van had already left for Cleveland, where Azalea Holdings, LLC had helped him find and purchase a new bar. Carmen got into the passenger side of the Grand Cherokee while Lucky took a last look around. He was standing there in the chill air with his #7 Ben Roethlisberger jersey clutching his skin. This town and the bar had so many memories for him. He kissed his hand and made like to blow a kiss to the bar, but instead, he hiked a leg and slapped his ass. "Fuck you, Nevileville," he yelled with tears in his eyes. He raised up two middle fingers, first at the bar and then at the river. "Fuck you," he whispered.

# The Jerk at the Top of the Stairs

<u>1</u>

Mackenzie Young and Billie Stephenson lived in a first-floor apartment on River Road, just down from their friend Tink and from the business section of Nevileville.  Business section was a stretch, as it was just a village river town.  There was The Periodic Coffee House, Miss America Pies, Lucky's Bar, Edna's Antiques, Jenny's Salon, Sizemore Meats, and A Portal Through Pages book store.

Mac, as she was called, was a poet and an English teacher at the Nevileville Middle School.  She was published in a few magazines, just a $100 payout here and there, but she was collecting her poems in hopes of getting the collection published in book form.  She also did freelance writing for greeting cards for the National Card Company.  She had helped usher in a new genre of cards for the LGBT community, which was a hit for National.

Mac's partner, Billie, was a forklift operator in a warehouse in Cincinnati by day, and a professional wrestler by night.  She went back the name of Veronica Valhalla and dressed like a Viking, complete with plastic breastplate, horned helmet, and blond wig.  She looked like Thor, if Thor was a woman, although about 60 pounds heavier.

Mac and Billie had been together for four years and had been living in the apartment together for the last three.  They had met at a Taste of Cincinnati event, where multitudes of food and beer vendors were set up downtown.  This was an annual event attended by tens of thousands, including Mac and her artist friends.  One of the attractions at a Taste of Cincinnati was a series of wrestling matches.  The ring was set up right in the middle of all the vendors.  There was a railing around the ring but no chairs.  Patrons could stand at the railing with their craft beer and brat or Cincinnati-style chili or meander around and watch while they browsed.  Mac and her friends stopped to watch a midget wrestling match between El Dragon Pequeno and Trooper Jack, who looked like a tiny member of the Village People.  It was funny to watch the little guys bounce around the ring, but they were very talented.  They were acrobatic and performed several top rope moves.  Trooper Jack won the match after he blinded El Dragon Pequeno by turning his mask around so his eye holes were at the back of his head.  The crowd laughed and cheered as Jack sauntered around the ring doing pelvic thrusts.

Lucian "Frenchy" Wilhelm was bored and was ready to take off to find "culture," but Mac wanted to watch more of the show.  Jay and Tink stayed behind with Mac, while Frenchy, Jenny, and Pete went to find their friend Sireen, who would be performing acoustic folk music on the Hoff's Beer Stage in half an hour.

The next match was an inter-gender match between a muscle-bound guy dressed like a surfer named Hang Ten Tim and a massive Viking woman called Veronica Valhalla.  Her arms were bigger than Hang Ten's, and he didn't stand a chance.  When the bell rang, he did a cart wheel in front of Valhalla and held his arms wide in a "What do you think of that?" gesture.  Veronica clotheslined his ass.  She picked him up off the mat by his hair while he gasped for breath.  Veronica easily hoisted him up on her shoulders and twirled, giving him the old airplane spin.  Herself dizzy, Valhalla dropped Tim to the mat then proceeded to the turnbuckle. The onlookers gasped as she climbed not to the second rope but all the way to the top. Raising her head and her right hand high, Valhalla yelled, "For Odin!" and leapt off the turnbuckle, giving Hang Ten Tim a devastating frog splash. With Tim lying motionless, the referee quickly counted to three, but that wasn't enough for Veronica. She insisted the referee count to ten, which he did. The bell rang, and the referee raised Veronica Valhalla's hand in victory. As Mac cheered and clapped, Valhalla looked over at her and gave her a wink. She got out of the ring, came right over to Mac, grabbed the bratwurst right out of Mac's hand, and took a huge bite. She nodded at Jay and Tink, winked again at Mac, and left the ring area with Mac's brat.

Jay and Tink reminded Mac about Sireen's set, and Mac reluctantly walked away with them. Sireen Wells, who just went by "Sireen" on stage, was a powerhouse vocalist and pretty good guitarist. It was at this event that Sireen would get noticed and would end up recording four albums and tour worldwide, mostly at festivals. Her set opened with Joni Mitchell's "Big Yellow Taxi." Sireen followed that with Melissa Etheridge's "I'm the Only One" and Jewel's "Angel Standing By." The crowd cheered, and Sireen addressed the crowd. "How's everybody doing tonight?" Cheers. "This song is an oldie and a personal favorite of mine. I have to ask you all something. Don't you want somebody to love?" The crowd went wild as Sireen played her folksy rendition of the Jefferson Airplane classic. As Mac was singing along, she heard a husky voice in her ear. "Thanks for the brat." She turned her head and saw the Viking standing next to her, without her blonde wig. She was a head taller than Mac and she had long brown hair instead of Nordic blond.

"You're welcome," Mac stammered. "How did you find me?"

"I've been looking all over for you," Veronica said. "I'm Billie."

"Mackenzie," she replied, "but my friends call me Mac."

Sireen kept singing, belting out the chorus. "Don't you want somebody to love? Don't you need somebody to love? Wouldn't you love somebody to love? You better find somebody to love."

"Don't you?" Billie asked.

"Don't I what?" Mac replied.

Billie looked down into Mac's hazel eyes. "Want somebody to love?"


**<u>2</u>**


Billie and Mac dated for a year before they decided to move in together. They decided to live in Mac's apartment since it was close to Mac's work and her friends. Billie didn't have any ties, so it didn't matter where she lived. Her family had disowned her eight years earlier when she told them she was gay. It still pained her, but she used that rage in her wrestling matches. Whenever an opponent was getting the best of her, Billie used that negative energy and made it a positive by beating the snot out of them.

Mac had warned Billie about their upstairs neighbor, Mr. Franks. Henry Franks was an elderly gentleman, mid 70s with a full head of silver hair. He was not a friendly man. Mac had tried to be nice to him, but he always seemed standoffish. At every holiday, Mac would buy a pie from Miss American Pies and take it to him.  Pumpkin pie at Thanksgiving, pecan pie at Christmas, cherry pie at Valentine's Day, and apple pie for the 4th of July.  She would walk the pie up the stairs and knock on his door.  After the third knock, Franks would open the door, with the chain still attached.

"Mr. Franks?" Mac always started.  "I brought you a pie.  Happy ____."

Franks would scowl, unchain the door, and open it.  He was always wearing a robe and basketball shorts, though she never knew him to shoot hoops.  He always had two-day stubble on his face.  Franks would take the pie from her, grumble a thank you, and shut the door.  Mac would always shake her head and walk down the stairs to her apartment.

Mr. Franks didn't like noise.  Anytime the music was too loud, or things were too loud in the bedroom, Franks would bang a broom handle on the floor.  Mac and Billie would hear it, and they would tone things down.  A little.  He especially didn't like it when Mac's friends came over.  One time he called the police because they were all outside while Billie was cooking chicken on the grill.  The smell of the chicken was coming in through his window.  The cops arrived and found that there was nothing illegal going on.  In fact, the two officers stayed and had a piece of chicken and corn on the cob with the group.  Mac even took a plate up to Mr. Franks, but he refused to open the door.

Mac's friends, and even Billie, wondered why Mac tried so hard.  Mac would just shrug and say that he was a lonely old man, and she was trying to do her part to be a good neighbor and to make her little part of the world a better place.  Her friends would always call him "Mr. Weiner" or "Franks and Beans," behind his back, but Mac would chide them, even though she thought the reference to "There's Something About Mary" was hilarious.


## 3


Mac took her last pie to Mr. Franks on February 14, 2018. It was a cherry pie.  He answered the door on the third knock.

"Mr. Franks?  Happy Valentine's Day."

Mr. Franks unchained the door and took the pie.  He grumbled thanks and started to close the door.

"Wait, Mr. Franks?"

"What is it?"  he snarled.

"I just wanted to let you know that Billie and I are moving in April.  Our lease is up, and we've been hearing about a company buying up property here.  I took a job teaching in Dayton."

"Well, good luck to you then," Franks said, closing the door.  Mac shrugged then turned and walked downstairs.

Mac and Billie found a house in the Dayton area and made an offer that was accepted by the seller.  At the end of March, they were busy packing, and boxes covered their living room floor.  As they were taping and labelling boxes, there came a knock on their door. Mac answered the door and was surprised to see Mr. Franks standing there with a pie in his hand.  It smelled like blueberry.  He was wearing a pair of gray slacks and a red sweater.

"Mr. Franks?  What a pleasant surprise," Mac announced.

"No, I'm sure it's not," he replied.  "I've been a very bad

neighbor."

Mac lied, "Oh, no, of course not."

Mr. Franks smiled, the first smile Mac had ever seen on his face, which was now clean shaven. "No need to tell a lie," he said. "I know how I've been, and I'd like to apologize. Please take this pie as a small token of appreciation."

"Mr. Franks, this is a Miss American Pie. They closed down three weeks ago."

"I know," he stated, shaking his head. "Such a shame. I bought the last pie they had and kept it in the freezer. I took it out this morning and warmed it up for you."

"That was very nice of you. Would you like to come in?" she asked.

"No," he replied. "You've been too kind to me already."

"Please, Mr. Franks? Mac begged. "Come in and have a slice of pie and a cup of coffee."

Mr. Franks looked up the stairs and then nodded his head. "Alright," he said.

Mac stepped back, and Mr. Franks entered the apartment. Billie was stunned to see him. "Mac? She started.

Mr. Franks smiled at her. "Hello, Billie," he said warmly. "I was just apologizing to Mackenzie. I owe you an apology as well. I'm sorry I've been so mean to you both, and to your friends."

"Yeah, well," Billie began.

Mac touched her arm and said, "No, Billie, it's okay. Mr.

Franks, would you like to sit down?" she said, gesturing to a small square table.

"Thank you," he said, sitting down.

"Billie, Mr. Franks brought us a pie."

"Please, call me Henry," the old man said.

"I see," Billie replied. "I'll make a pot of coffee."

Mac and Billie went into the kitchen to get plates, napkins, and forks. "What's going on?" Billie asked.

"I don't know," Mac replied, "But Mr. Franks is finally being nice, and I'm going to be nice, too."

"You're always nice," Billie said with a grin.

"Give him a chance," Mac said.

Billie brought three cups of coffee, spoons, sugar, and creamer to the table. "So, why have you been so mean to us all these years?"

"Billie!" Mac said, raising her voice.

"No, she's right," Henry replied. "I'm afraid I've been a very bad neighbor, and I am so very sorry. I never should have been so mean to you."

"Then why were you," Mac asked.

"I gave up on people a long time ago," he started. I was an actor. I moved to New York and performed on Broadway. It was only in the theater that I could openly be myself around other men. Do you know how hard it was to be a gay man in the '60s?

"Wait, you're gay?" Mac asked.

Henry smiled.  "Yes, don't let the robes and stubble fool you.  I used to be quite flamboyant.  That was a different time, and there were many men of money and power who would support a young man, if you know what I mean, but it was all a secret.  They all had wives and families and hid who they were."

"Where are you from, Henry?" Billie asked.

"I am originally from Birmingham, Alabama.  If you think they were prejudiced against blacks in the 50s and 60s, how do you think they felt about gays?"

"I understand," Billie said.

"No, you really don't," he said.  My parents didn't want me to be in plays or act.  My father wanted me to play football for Bear Bryant.  Wanted me to be a man and play for the Crimson Tide.  That really was not for me.  I finally had to tell my parents I was gay.  My father hit me, and my mother cried.  They kicked me out of their house with nothing except the clothes on my back and the $20 I had in my wallet.  I never saw them or my brothers again.  I hitchhiked as far as I could to save money.  I knew I wanted to act, so I went to New York.  I got a job on Broadway, but it was for sweeping the floor and cleaning the toilets.  I took it because I had nothing else.  I was able to watch the performances, though, and I learned from them.  One day while I was sweeping the stage, the director heard me singing the lines to one of the songs in the musical.  He liked what he heard and wanted to hear more, in his office.  I did what I felt I needed to do, and he offered me a supporting role in the musical.  Eventually I was cast in lead roles, but it was always the same.  I would have to sleep with the producer or service a wealthy donor to get a good role.  I did that for almost 15 years before I became "too old" for the producers and donors.  They wanted younger men and boys.  Fresh meat, they said.  I left New York and became a drama teacher at a high school in Morgantown, West Virginia.  Big mistake.  If I thought they hated gays in Alabama, West Virginia was much worse.  They were all blue-collar miners, hillbillies, and moonshine drinkers.  I was there for 4 years.  A group of miners found out that I was gay.  I was seeing one of the other miners, and they caught us one night in his hunting cabin.  He had a wife and kids, too.  They beat me up as a lesson to their friend and told him if he didn't get back to his wife and stop being a fag, they were going to kill him.  They basically ran me out of town, and I ran for the next 20 years.  I went all over the country, teaching in Michigan, Indiana, Oregon, and Las Vegas.  I finally got tired of running and moved here.  I ran the opera house for a few years, but it wasn't an opera house then.  I fixed it up and converted it into a second-run movie theater.  It did well for the first couple of years because there were no other movie theaters around the area.  Everyone had to go up to the city to see a film.  The last big flood, back in 2008, caused a lot of damage to the theater.  The claim adjusters also found asbestos, and the building was condemned.  I didn't have money or the energy to get it abated, so I sold it to some investment company for a pretty sizable profit last year.  Nobody would touch it before then because of the asbestos.  So, here I am now, living off the sale of the opera house, mad at the world for not accepting me and for me not having the courage to accept myself."

Billie and Mac each took one of Henry's hands.

"We do understand, Henry," Mac said.  "Especially Billie."

Henry look at Billie.  "You do?"

"I do.  My family disowned me and kicked me out 8 years ago," she said as she wiped away a tear.  "I haven't talked to them since.  I was pissed off at the world, too, until I met Mac."

Henry and Billie both looked at Mac and smiled.  "She's a

good egg," Henry said.

They talked for a while longer, each having another piece of pie.  When the pie was gone, Henry stood up.  "I know y'all are busy, and I'm going to get out of your hair.  He gave Billie and Mac each a hug, and he kissed Mac on the cheek.  "Thank you for not giving up on an old man."

"You're welcome, Henry," she replied.  Henry opened the door and started out.  "Henry?" she asked.

Mr. Franks turned back around.  "Yes?"

"You know that investment company you talked about?"

"Of course."

"Do you know they're buying up other properties around here?"

"I do.  My lease is up in June, and the landlord has already told me he's not renewing."

"Oh," Mac said.  "What will you do?"

"In think I'm going to pack up and move back to Birmingham.  It's been a long time since I saw my brothers.  Do you think they'll accept me now?"

Billie walked over to him and patted him on the back.  "If they don't, you let me know, old man, and I'll come down there and chokeslam them!"

Henry laughed.  "I think that might wise them up," he said, closing the door behind him.

They heard him trudge back up the stairs.  Billie took Mac into her arms and gave her a kiss.  "You don't give up on people, do you?"

"With everything else going on in the world, what people need is other people to listen to them and love them. You never know what kind of change you can make just by being nice to someone."

"Well," Billie said, giving Mac another squeeze, "I know what kind of change you made on 'Franks and Beans,' and I know what kind of change you made in me. Let's finish packing and go make a change in Dayton. If your kindness won't change them, my chokeslams will."

Billie kissed her again. Mac felt warm and safe in her arms. Mr. Franks would be okay now. The world was a little bit brighter today.

# Posted:  No Trespassing

Wyman Ellerman lived by himself in an old cabin in the woods across the highway from the village of Nevileville.  Cabin was an exaggeration.  Hell, shack was an exaggeration.  It was really more of a hovel, but it was all Wyman needed.  He had a wood-burning stove to cook on and to keep warm, and there were plenty of trees that kept dropping limbs, so he was set for firewood.  He had a couple of pairs of work pants that he kept stitched, a couple of flannel shirts and a heavy jacket for the winter and a few short sleeve shirts for the spring and summer.  He also had his Bible, a fishing pole, a pocket knife, and an axe.  What more could a man really need?

During the day he would walk along the stream that ran by his place, casting a line here and there to catch fish.  Sometimes he would walk through the village and fish in the river.  If he had a really good catch, Mr. Sizemore at the butcher shop would trade pork or chicken for some fish, sometimes beef if the catch was really good.  Wyman had a small garden behind his cabin where he grew a few tomatoes and some potatoes.  There were some wild blackberries and strawberries in the woods, so he generally had enough to eat.  When he didn't there were always the worms.

At night, Ellerman would sit by the wood-burning stove and read his Bible, a few verses every night.  One of his favorite lines was found in Luke 12:15.  It read, "The he said to them, 'Watch out!  Be on your guard against all kinds of greed; life does not consist in an abundance of possession.'"  Those were words to live by.  When he was finished reading, Wyman would take out his pocket knife and pick out a nice block of wood. He would sit with his back against the wall and whittle away at the wood. When he slept, Ellerman would lay his head on an old shirt that had been stuffed with leaves.

Not many people in Nevileville still read the Good Book. Jesus left the last church around 1972. Folks in Nevileville had their own thoughts, which didn't necessarily make them bad people. There were still a few that went to church, just not in Nevileville. Wyman didn't mind. His church was in the woods, and he had his Bible. Jesus was all around him, in every blade of grass, in every fallen leaf, in the fish he caught, and in the sunlight that came down through the trees.

Everybody in the village knew Wyman Ellerman or knew about him. They thought he was just a crazy middle-aged man. Perhaps he was. Maybe he wasn't, but they knew to stay out of his woods. Technically, it wasn't his woods, and it wasn't even his cabin, but it's where he lived, and no one else laid claim to it. Squatter's rights.

Wyman had money, enough to get by anyway. He could have had more, but he didn't need it, so he gave it away, mostly to the orphanage, but also some to other children's causes or to veterans.

Nobody knew exactly where Ellerman came from, and neither did he. Some speculated that his mother was from Kentucky, but no one really knew for sure. He was about two years old when he was left at the orphanage. He just walked in the front door with a note pinned to a dirty t-shirt. He was wearing blue jeans with holes in the knees. His feet were bare. The note simply read:

"Please take care of the boy. I can't."

That was it.  No name or anything else.  The note was written on a piece of cardboard torn from a box.  The people at the orphanage asked him his name, but the boy just shook his head.  They asked him his mother's name.  He just shook his head.  His father's name?  Where he lived?  Who brought him to the orphanage?  The boy simply shook his head.  He either didn't know how to speak, couldn't speak, or didn't want to speak.  This was in 1940.

The orphanage brought in Dr. McNichols to give the boy a physical.  There were no cuts or bruises on the boy, but there were old marks on his legs that looked like cigarette burns.

The staff at the orphanage didn't know what to do with the boy.  They couldn't just call him "boy."  There was no way to know where he came from.  He could have been from Ohio, Kentucky, Indiana, or anywhere else.  The mother could have been passing through and decided to leave him.

After a lot if discussions, the staff decided to pick his name out of a hat.  They put about fifty first names into a hat and Sylvia Goodling, the receptionist, drew a name.  He could have been Richard, Thomas, Benjamin, or a host of other names, but the name selected was Wyman, the name of a famous minor league baseball player from Maysville.  The same thing happened with the last name.  They picked surnames that were not associated with residents of the village, and, of course, Ellerman was the one picked.  Once the name was selected, they brought the boy into the office and told him his name was Wyman Ellerman.  When asked if he liked the name, little Wyman just shrugged.

Over the next few months, the staff took care of Wyman, carefully working with the boy, teaching him words, reading him books, and showing him how to play with toys.  The first present Wyman received was a Bible, a gift from the reverend at the

Calvary Baptist Church.  Wyman couldn't read yet, and it wasn't a children's Bible, but it did have illustrations throughout the book.  There was a depiction of the angel with the flaming sword at the Garden of Eden.  There was an illustration of the Burning Bush, the Tower of Babel, and Noah's Ark.  There were maps of the Holy Land.  There were pictures of Jesus getting baptized by John the Baptist, Jesus turning water to wine, Jesus feeding the masses, Jesus walking on water, Jesus and the disciples at the Last Supper, and Jesus hanging on a cross.  There were pictures of Mary at the opened tomb of Christ, and there were depictions of the Four Horsemen of the Apocalypse.  Wyman spent a lot of time looking at the pictures.  When he closed his eyes at night, he could see them clearly in his mind.  Sometimes he had nightmares about the Four Horsemen, and he'd wake up in a sweat.

Wyman grew and learned at the orphanage.  He was enrolled in kindergarten when he was 5.  Sylvia would walk him to school in the mornings and walk him back to the orphanage in the afternoon.  He had trouble adjusting to school because it was a more structured environment.  The kids all looked nicer and dressed nicer.  Although the orphanage took good care of him, there wasn't much of a budget for clothes, and Wyman wore hand-me-downs.

There was a carousel of kids that passed through the orphanage.  Most didn't stay long.  Some kids were fostered out, and others were lucky to be adopted.  Initially the head of the orphanage, Randolph Cason, was afraid to foster Wyman, as he did not want the child to feel abandoned again.  Most couples that came in looking to adopt were interested in finding a baby, not a 5-year-old.  It really didn't matter to Wyman.  The orphanage was his home.

As the years progressed, Ellerman began to be bullied at the elementary and junior high schools.  The kids were cruel and made fun of how he looked, how he dressed, and the fact that he had no parents.  By then, Wyman could read well and had read the Bible several times.  He knew how to turn the other cheek, even though it hurt inside.  He wouldn't add fuel to the fire.

Most of the time he sat by himself at lunch.  Because of his status, he was given free lunch by the schools.  He was fond of sloppy Joe's and jello, especially the kind with the fruit floating around in it.  On the playground, he was often alone as well.  He would watch the other kids play tag or Red Rover, but he was never invited to join.  He usually sat on the steps and would read a book from the school's library.  Tom Swift, Edgar Rice Burroughs, H.G. Wells, H. Rider Haggard, and Jules Verne books were his favorites.  Back at the orphanage in the afternoons, Wyman would act out what he had read that day after he finished his chores.  He was in charge of making his bed each day, sweeping his floor and the kitchen and dining room floors, and washing dishes after supper.  He didn't mind.  He took pride in doing a good job, and he could daydream while he worked.

When he was 16, the orphanage arranged for him to work after school with the Recreation and Parks Department.  After school and on weekends, Wyman would help cut grass, trim bushes and trees, make general repairs, and help maintain the baseball and football fields.  It was good work, and Wyman enjoyed being outside in the sun.  He didn't even mind having to work while the other kids played baseball in their white uniforms.  He would stop and watch them from time to time, not because he was envious but because he wanted to learn.  He watched and learned everything he could.  A lot of folks presumed that he was stupid or slow because he was an orphan, but Wyman Ellerman was very intelligent.  Most people didn't know because most people wouldn't take the time to talk to him.

Wyman went to church on Sundays.  The village still had

churches at that time, and Wyman always sat in the back row of Calvary Baptist Church, where he would listen to Reverend Jacobs' sermons and sing along with the congregation on "The Old Rugged Cross," "Shall We Gather at the River," "The Garden," and countless others.  Sometimes when he worked, Wyman would sing or hum these hymns to himself.  He didn't really know any of the popular music since he didn't have a radio at the orphanage, but he had heard the kids at school talking about "The King" Elvis Presley.  The only king Wyman knew was Jesus.

Wyman offered the money he made to the orphanage, but Cason wouldn't accept it.  He took Wyman down to the Bank of Nevileville and helped him open a savings account.  Wyman did not have any identification, other than his school records, so Cason signed for him.  Each week when Wyman got paid in cash from the rec department, he would go to the bank and deposit it all except for fifty cents, which he would put in the collection plate at church.

After he turned 18 and graduated from high school, the orphanage was forced to make Wyman leave.  It was a sad day for Wyman, and for the staff at the orphanage, who had come to know and love him.  This was the only home he ever knew, and he had considered Mr. Cason as a father and Mrs. Goodling as a mother.  As Wyman was the only child left at the orphanage and because of new laws being implemented in Ohio, the orphanage would be closing down.  Cason retired and moved to North Carolina.  Goodling was elderly and was in a nursing home by then.  Ellerman had no real place to go.  He briefly thought about leaving Nevileville, hoboing a train and just going wherever it took him, but the thought scared him.  Since he was 2, Nevileville had been his home.

Vincent Truman, the head of the maintenance crew for the rec department, offered to let Wyman stay in one of the maintenance buildings.  It smelled like grass and oil, but it was roomy enough, and dry.  Truman set Wyman up with a cot, and that's where he lived for the next 4 years.  Wyman had money saved up in the bank, but he was used to meager living, and the idea of an apartment didn't suit him.  He liked living in the maintenance building, where he could tinker with the small engines on the lawn mowers and fiddle with the tools.

Wyman was an early riser, and he was up and dressed by six am most days.  His work day began at eight, so he would make himself oatmeal and go for a walk through the village and surrounding areas.  One morning he crossed the highway adjacent to the village and began walking through the woods.  About a quarter mile into the woods, there was what appeared to be an old log hunting cabin next to Willow Creek.  It was dilapidated and looked as if it had not been in use for a long time.  He tried the door and it opened easily, nearly falling off.  It was small inside and damp.  There were old newspapers lying around on the floor, and mice had made their beds among them.  The tin roof was falling in, and the one window was broken.

Wyman asked Vincent if he knew anything about the cabin, but Vincent had no idea.  He helped Wyman check the land records, and it was found to be property of the village, but there were no records of any cabin there.  Vincent helped Ellerman broker a deal with the mayor to lease the land and cabin there for $10 a year.  No, the fee wasn't much, but the village couldn't just have him living on their land for free.  One of the clauses in the lease stated that Wyman could not build any new structure on the property.  That didn't mean he couldn't fix up the old cabin.

Before and after work each day, Wyman would go to the cabin.  He started off by cleaning up the inside, removing all the trash and the mice.  The he fixed any holes so that no more mice or snakes could get inside.  He mended the roof so it wouldn't leak, and he cleaned all the mold and mildew from the wood inside.

Eventually he was able to get a piece of glass to repair the broken window. By withdrawing some of his savings from the bank, Wyman was able to purchase a wood-burning stove. Vincent drove the stove over to the edge of the woods and helped Wyman get it to the cabin. After about three months, the cabin was livable, and Wyman moved in.

There was no bathroom or outhouse and no running water, so Ellerman did his business in the woods. He would bathe himself in the creek when it was warm. When it was cold, he would heat up water on the stove and wash himself off in the cabin with a cloth.

He had no pictures on the walls, but Wyman would take to drawing Bible scenes on the walls with charcoal from the stove. He would also jot down Bible verses or bits of poetry on the walls as well. Some of the poetry was his own. They weren't elaborate poems, just simple verse. Most were just a couple of lines, like, "My Lord, My Jesus. I see Your glory in the trees and in the stream. Let me bathe in Your light," and "The river is a song, and she sings of change. She washes the sin to the ocean, cleansing as she goes. I bathe in her, and I am new."

Wyman never knew a woman. There were women he would talk to in passing in the village or sometimes at church, but there was no one who interested him in that way, nor was he interesting in that way to any of the village women. He was not an unattractive man, but people generally didn't feel at ease in his presence. Everyone knew of Wyman, and most people felt he was beneath them.

He was employed by the Recreation Department for 50 years, doing the same jobs as he had when he was 16. He still cut the grass and worked on the mowers. He still trimmed trees and would chalk the baseball foul lines. When he retired, they threw him a small party with cake and ice cream.  The mayor wanted to give him a gold watch, but the folks at the rec department knew he'd never wear it.  Instead, they gave him a new fishing pole and a new pocket knife.  That was good enough for Wyman.  There was no pension for him.  He still had no identification.  No driver's license, no social security card, no birth certificate.  The village had paid him under the table for 50 years.  He wasn't officially on their books, other than on the original lease that he had signed back in 1957.

Even though he was a little over a half a mile from the village, Wyman made fewer and fewer walks through town.  He ate less and lived mostly off his fish, tomatoes, and potatoes.  He had learned to can some of them to have during the lean winter months.

No one came to visit Ellerman.  Years back, Wyman had placed a few signs up around the woods to keep out trespassers.  The signs were basic and read, "POSTED:  NO TRESPASSING."  It was more a deterrent than anything else.  It wasn't that he disliked people or didn't want anyone to visit, but there had been a few instances over the years where kids would come and vandalize the cabin.  Some young lovers would break in while he was working in the village and do what young lovers do.

In the winter of 2015, Wyman was laying on the floor of his cabin.  He was trying to sleep, but the coughing kept him awake.  He was feverish and cold at the same time.  He had been sick for a week, and the old wood-burning stove had finally died.  A newer model would never have lasted that long.  There was snow on the ground.  Wyman only knew because he had seen the snow falling out his window.  He was too ill to get up.  He had been able to make a little tomato soup yesterday, and he had a little left in a cup beside him.  It was cold, but he tried to drink it.  The acid burned his throat, and it looked like blood on his lips.  It was

November 17.  A week before Thanksgiving.  It was Wyman's actual birthday, but he didn't know it.  They had always celebrated his birthday on January 1 at the orphanage.  He was 77.

Wyman was amazed to hear a low knock on his door.  In a feeble voice, he called out, "Help me."  It was the only time in his life that he had asked for help.

"Get up, Wyman," he heard a voice say from outside.

"I cannot," he replied.

"Get up, Wyman," the voice said again with authority.

Surprisingly, Ellerman found that he could get up, but with difficulty.  He trudged to the door and unlocked it.  When he opened the door, the cold air hit him like a freight train, forcing him to stagger back.  There was no one there, and there were no footprints in the snow.  He began to close the door, thinking he was delusional from the fever.

"Come to me," he heard.

Wyman looked in the direction of the voice and saw a man near the creek bed.  Despite the weather, the man was wearing a green t-shirt and shorts.  The man waved him forward.  Wyman stepped out into the cold and sloshed through the snow.  He looked down and saw that he was leaving footprints, but the man in front of him had not.  As Wyman looked on, the man stepped into the creek.  The water level was high, up to the man's waist.  He motioned for Wyman to follow him in.

"I know You, my Lord," Wyman said.  "but it's too cold," he yelled over the wind and snow.

"If you know me," the man said, "then come to me."

"I know You, my Lord," Wyman repeated, stepping into the frigid water. It was like thousands of needles piercing his skin at once, but then the pain subsided. The water was warm, like a bath. The man took Wyman's hand.

"Wyman Ellerman," the man started. "I baptize you in the name of the Father, the Son, and the Holy Ghost." He reached out to Wyman's head and immersed him in the waters of Willow Creek. "You are free from sin, and your service is over. Well done, my son."

Two days later, Thom Meyers from the recreation department came through the woods looking for Wyman. No one had seen or heard from him in over two weeks. He came upon the cabin and knew something was wrong when he saw the door open. He went inside, but Wyman was not there. Looking around, Thom saw the footprints leading from the cabin. There was one sets of prints, all leading from the cabin. None returning. Meyers followed the footprints down the path to the creek. The mud on the creek bed was disturbed, and there were no footprints on the other side of the creek.

Wyman Ellerman's body was never found. It was assumed that he had fallen into the creek and his body had made its way to the Ohio River. They set out a search party along the river but found no trace of Ellerman. He was declared legally dead, which was a bit of an issue, since there wasn't much of a record of him being alive.

At the Bank of Nevileville, Wyman Ellerman had a safe deposit box. In the box was a single document, Wyman's will. It was signed by J. Morgan Binghamton, the only lawyer in town. The will specified that the money in Ellerman's savings account be donated to the Nevileville Little League to use as needed. There was nearly $250,000 that Ellerman had saved in the 50 years he had worked for the Recreation and Parks Department, plus interest from the bank.

The Village of Nevileville and the Recreation and Parks Department dedicated the Little League baseball field to Wyman Ellerman, a man who had watched the boys play but who had never actually played the game himself.  Ellerman's money helped the team build new dugouts and buy new uniforms and bats.  The Little League would have been able to use that money for years, had Azalea Holdings, LLC not bought up the property around the village and turned it into a golf course.

While part of the village, Wyman Ellerman's cabin was outside of the scope for the golf course.  It sat forgotten in the woods across the highway from Rolling Mounds Golf Course. Course workers, professional golfers, and spectators passed by those woods every day, not knowing about Wyman Ellerman or his cabin in the woods.  Mice, spiders, and birds retook the cabin, bedding down under the eyes of a charcoal Jesus.

# The Day the Village Died

It was a chilly November morning, crisp but not quite cold. The snow would be coming in a few weeks, and there would be no plows to clear the roads. Not this year. Not ever again. The last few houses would be vacant in the next few hours. Moving vans, trucks and cars were being loaded.

Sam walked slowly down River Road. He stopped and looked in all the empty storefronts as he passed. The taps were all dry in Lucky's Bar. There were no bottles of gin and whiskey on the shelves. The tables, chairs, and barstools were all gone. The televisions that showed all the NFL and NBA games and the occasional UFC fight had been taken down. At A Portal Through Pages, all the books had been cleared off the shelves. Dickens, Hemingway, King, and all the Harlequins had been packed up. Some had been donated to thrift shops and some had been sold on eBay, but they were all gone. Jenny's Hair Salon was all dark. No more cuts and dye jobs there. Sam saw a roach crawling on the floor, and he moved on. The Miss American Pie Company was completely empty. The display cases that held pies of all flavors were gone. The menu board still hung on the wall behind the counter. It still listed the pies of the day: lemon meringue, apple cinnamon, strawberry/rhubarb, and coconut cream. $2.00/slice, $12.00/whole pie. Sam had sold a lot of these slices of pies in the coffeehouse after his mother had died and he took over the business from his dad, who just didn't have the heart for it a anymore. His mother had made all the baked goods before she passed.

Sam moved on past Chuck's Laundromat and Edna's Antiques. Both empty, like everything else. Finally, he came to The Periodic Coffee House. He sighed as he peered into the darkness. He had the key in his pocket, but he didn't want to go back inside. It was over. He saw the place where the large periodic table used to hang. You could see the outline on the wall. He had removed it, along with the picture of Gutterball that had hung on the wall and the picture of Lucy and her friend that had sat by the counter. He missed Lucy. She was quite a character, always changing her look and reinventing herself.

A stray dog ran past, not even giving Sam the time of day. He hoped someone would take it with them.

Sam sighed. He had grown up in this coffeehouse, setting up the chairs in the mornings before school, doing his homework at the table that had sat in the corner near the restroom. He remembered his mama humming Beach Boys and Motown songs as she baked in the kitchen. His dad would go in sometimes and grab his mother and they would have a quick dance while she hummed. He smiled as he thought about this. His dad would go around to each table when he had a moment. He would ask everyone how they were and if they needed anything else. If someone complimented the pie (which they always did), his dad would yell out, "Annabelle, they like your pie!" His mom would stick her head out the window between the counter and the kitchen and say thank you. So long ago, but it was like yesterday. Sam could really see them there. They were happy. He had been happy. He could see his daughter Laurel doing the same things he had done, helping set up, doing her homework at the same table in the corner. He could see his wife Kaitlyn waiting tables and making coffee drinks after Lucy passed. When they brought Noah into the world, they would place him in a playpen and he would play or sleep while they worked. He remembered the poetry nights they'd had.  Some had been very good with the spoken word.  Some not so good.  He remembered one poem in particular where everything rhymed with heart, including fart.  There had been history lectures here about the founders of the city, the history of the boats on the river, slavery and the role of abolitionists in the village, and the few celebrities and athletes that were from the village.  There had been acoustical acts that would come and play on the weekends and sometimes during the week after they'd started serving beer.  One famous country musician had played here once before he made it big.  There had been a lot of good times in the old coffeehouse.  Over 40 years of them.  Sam wanted to cry, but he stopped himself.  He still had things to do and a few more boxes to pack.

A car passed the coffeehouse, and the driver honked the horn.  It was Lucky.  Sam waved and watched the car go by, with his Pittsburgh Steelers flags attached to his windows, flapping in the breeze.  He was relocating to Cleveland, where he would still be an asshole.  The back of his car was loaded with bags and boxes.  A second car, driven by his wife, Carmen, rolled past.  She waved but did not honk.  Sam waved politely, and they were gone.

At the end of the road, a couple of bulldozers sat.  A crane would be in town in the next couple of days.  The golf course had bought up everything, and they were going to get as much done before the snows came.  The course wouldn't be ready for about a year and a half, but there were rumors that the PGA was already looking to hold a big tournament here.  After all, the owners already ran the most successful golf tournament on the planet.

A trailer had been set up in the vacant lot just down from the coffeehouse.  This was the construction trailer.  This was where the heavy equipment operators would get their marching orders.  It looked out of place here in the village, but then again, this was no longer a village.  He would miss this, all of it.  He was going to take the large amount of money he had been offered for the coffeehouse, his house, and his parents' house, and they were going someplace warm.  Somewhere with a beach.  They had made a lot of memories here, but they would make new ones, in a new place.

Sam took a piece of pink sidewalk chalk out of his pocket and knelt by the door of the coffeehouse.  He drew a big pink heart and wrote "Keller" inside it.  Above the heart he wrote, "I love you…periodically."

A tear started to form in his right eye, but he wiped it away. The tears would come to all of them but not yet.  Not until later. Not until the people were settled into their new homes, their new jobs, their new lives.  Not until the bulldozers and cranes demolished the roads and buildings.  When the village was gone for good and the landscaping started, that is when the tears would come, when people realized that what they'd had was gone forever. There was no going home.

Sam heard a boat horn and saw a riverboat going down the river.  He turned to watch it go by.  The River Bandit.  That was the name on the side of the boat.  It was a fitting name, since everything had been stolen from them.  Not truly stolen, not truly taken, but in the end, it was the same. When enough of the village had sold off, there wasn't anything left to do. As he watched the boat, a man with long brown hair and a beard stepped out on the deck.  He might have been wearing a green shirt, but it was hard to tell at this distance.  The man had a coffee cup in his left hand, and he took a sip.  He looked directly at Sam and raised the cup in a sign of hello.  Sam raised a hand back.  The men looked at each for a moment, then the man turned to face downriver.  Sam had a feeling that he had seen this man somewhere before, and it was surely possible, since riverboats were on the Ohio all the time. There was something else, though, but Sam couldn't quite put his finger on it.

Sam turned back towards home.  The family was almost packed up, but he'd wanted one last goodbye.  He made a quacking sound, and immediately the quack was returned.  Gutterball came waddling around from the back of the coffeehouse, followed by a brown female duck.  Laurel had started calling her Lane to keep in the bowling theme.  Behind the two ducks came group of six ducklings, their little feet moving fast to keep up with their parents.  Despite the sadness, Sam had to laugh.  He was going to need a bigger box.

# **Historical Marker**

The Village of Nevileville, Ohio ceased to exist on November 4, 2018.  It was on that day that the last residents moved out of town and Azalea Holdings, LLC had taken over ownership of the entire village.  They wasted no time.  The day before, Nevileville fire, police, and EMT services had executed a house-by-house and building-by-building search to make sure that people or animals were still inside.  This took the better part of the day, and fortunately everyone was gone.  Demolition began at 7:30 AM on the 4th, after the foreman had conducted a tool box safety talk with all the workers.

It took several months to tear down, install sprinkler systems, increase the height of the levee, add fill dirt and sod, transplant trees and bushes, build clubhouses and outbuildings, and create parking lots, but finally, in February 2020, Rolling Mounds Golf Course was completed.  The first golf tournament was held there from May 14-17, 2020.  It was a collegiate tournament featuring several Midwest and northern schools such as the University of Cincinnati, Ohio State University, Marshall, and Purdue University.  The tournament was won by Wright State University.  The first professional tournament was an LPGA event held June 25-28 of that same year.  The winner was a 16-year-old Japanese golfer named Hasuke Yorimoto.  She would become the women's equivalent of Tiger Woods.  The first men's tournament was called The Greater Ohio Open and was held August 6-10.  Spaniard Juan Miguel Jimenez was the winner of the first tournament and would earn a spot in 2021's most prestigious event, The Masters.  The Greater Ohio Open would become one of the top tournaments on the PGA tour and was unofficially considered the fifth major.

Other than the memorial tributes placed around the course grounds, the only notification that this area had been anything other than a golf course was near the entrance to Rolling Mounds on the highway. It was an Ohio Historical Marker, which read:


OHIO

HISTORICAL

MARKER

THE VILLAGE OF NEVILEVILLE

The Village of Nevileville was founded at this location in 1804 by Josiah Nevile. The village was a prosperous river town during the 1800s with riverboat docks, hotels, and an opera house. The village was known as a stop on the Underground Railroad. Numerous escaped slaves found refuge in the village as they moved North. The village of Nevileville was unincorporated in the fall of 2018 and the land was purchased to create Rolling Mounds Golf Course. The village of Nevileville ceased to exist on November 4, 2018.

# As I Walked by the River, A Conclusion

As I walked by the river,

All the beauty that I'd seen

Had been replaced by fairways,

Water hazards, roughs, and greens.

And the geese and all the ducks

Have found other homes

And the peacock left also,

No more streets he roams.

The skies are still azure,

And the sun still reflects.

The river gleams; our Savior

Our dear town no more protects.

The pinks, the oranges, the yellows

On the storefronts are no more

In their place, magnolia scents,

And azaleas keeping score.

No more picnics or movies,

No concerts or Shakespeare plays,

The only game that's played now

Has a club, a ball, fairways.

There was nothing like our village,

Full of wonder, filled with pride

Now our Nevileville is gone,

River's full of tears we cried.

# ABOUT THE AUTHOR

Steve Cain is originally from Augusta, Georgia and now makes his home in New Richmond, Ohio with his wife, Theresa, his kids, Samantha and Ethan, three dogs, a cat, and a plethora of deer and turkeys. He is a Certified Safety Professional by day. His first book, *The Great Inevitable,* was published in 2019 through Losantiville Press. His other books are available on Amazon or through the author. He is also the lead singer for the heavy metal band, Critical Khaos. You can connect with Steve on Facebook (Steve Cain Writer), on Twitter (@stevecainwriter), and on Instagram (19stevecain72). If you enjoy his writing, please leave a review on Amazon and Goodreads. Thank you!